Remnants from the Fire

A Transformational Journey with the Archetypes

By

Lark Aleta Ferguson

ISBN: 0-7596-9631-4 (Electronic)
ISBN: 0-7596-9632-2 (Softcover)

This book is printed on acid free paper.

1st Books - rev. 05/24/02

Acknowledgements

I am forever grateful for the help I have received through the process of getting this book to its finished version.

My first note of gratitude goes to my earliest mentor and guide, my brother Bill Batey, both for his timely suggestion that set me on the road to discovery and for the long hours of discussion that helped me along my way.

I appreciate the support and encouragement I have received from my husband Bob and for his editing and grammatical suggestions and his willingness to turn the Mac over to me to do the project. Thanks, I couldn't have finished the book without you. You have kept your promise to be the protector of my solitude and so much more.

To Sue Ostergardt I owe a big debt of gratitude for her notes and grammatical suggestions. Her help with the editing was very much appreciated, as well as her comments and suggestions on the story itself.

To June Eddinger I offer a multitude of thanks for being willing to read the story she knows so well and offer her suggestions.

To my sister Lydia, whose suggestion of reading Steven King's book on writing became a valuable resource as I began the job of cleaning up the manuscript for publication. Thanks Lydia.

To my sister Cindy Albers, also a budding writer, I owe my appreciation for giving me some suggestions on the order of the story that worked much better than the original manuscript.

Finally, the direction my development took would not have been possible without The Prince. I appreciate his soul, even though I can't get along with the person. I have heard it said that it takes a very strong connection to someone to have the power to make life difficult enough to make that person grow. I think that was his agreement with me.

To the many teachers I have "sat at the feet" of through their books, I am forever grateful for the works that became my companions on a journey that took me almost 30 years.

Through the hard work of distillation, I was able to explore the terrain of my psyche and find my own voice.

There were too many books and teachers for me to list, but a few were turning points, sending me down an entirely different road than I had traveled before. These I mention:

I am grateful to the Seth Material, my first venture into the world of consciousness exploration. Seth helped me move outside the box of beliefs. His information had enormous impact on my curious and searching mind. (Seth was channeled through Jane Roberts in the 60's and 70's. She died in 1984 of a lingering illness. She channeled the material that produced at least 19 books from Seth as well as writing a few novels and other material. The Seth material is profoundly provocative and timeless.)

My Love to Lazaris and to Jach Purcell for being willing to give so much of his time and weekends to channel Lazaris. Lazaris helped me to take all that I had learned and put it to practical use with the many techniques They taught for creating my own reality . With Their love to guide me I discovered indescribable worlds and concepts. (See Chapter notes at end of this book, under Prologue for information about Lazaris.)

I am very grateful to Leslie Temple Thurston, for her willingness to go through so much to become enlightened. She is a modern prototype of what is possible for humanity. Her example has been a great source of inspiration to me, and thousands of modern seekers. She came into my life as a teacher after the time that is covered by this book. Studying with her helped me to believe that what I had learned and experienced held some value. I wrote most of this book during the time I was her student.

(Corelight, 223 North Guadalupe Street, PMB 275, Santa Fe, New Mexico 87501 sponsors Leslie's Teacher Training Courses, as well as other retreats and publications.)

Dedication

In memory of

Cherie Michelle Meents

1967-1984

TABLE OF CONTENTS

Fermentation

"Fermentation is flooding the mind with meaningful and
profoundly real images from something
totally beyond us that lies at the edge of our personal
reality. It is like a swinging door between one level of
consciousness and another, between soul and spirit,
between matter and mind."

The Seven Steps of Transformation

Dennis William Hauck The Emerald Tablet

INTRODUCTION

The "kingdom of God is within." How often have we heard that statement. The question becomes great idea but how do we access that "Kingdom" that is supposed to be somewhere within? For a world that is taught to look outside of itself for the answers, or to a religious leader, the statement sounds interesting but hardly practical. How do we access that kingdom within and utilize it?

The book you have in your hands is an autobiographical fantasy, and an experiential illustration of a process that I used as a tool to discover and explore that place inside myself that seemed so mysterious and hard to reach, my own "kingdom within."

My young adult life was similar in many ways to the lives of women who grew up in the 50's everywhere; believing in the promise of love, waiting for the handsome prince who would come and whisk me away to live happily ever after as we played "house" behind the white picket fence. What it became was a balancing act between adversity and joy of varying degrees mixed with the expectations my world projected onto me as a woman.

The story is one of love and loss, coupled with shame and guilt, as well as a story of recovery and hope, as I gradually learned how to escape from the painful prison of my beliefs.

The year was 1978, and I was in trouble. Struggling under the facade of a "happy marriage," up to my neck in emotional pain and rage, I began my long journey by turning to books for help. I read everything I could get my hands on, along the lines of self-help, alternative medicine, transpersonal psychology and metaphysics. One book would point me in the direction of another, and slowly I began to build a foundation of psychological and spiritual concepts. The building took years and was done in snatches between the interminable chores and events of raising a large family.

My studies began to shake loose the substructure of everything I had been taught to believe in. Then issues from childhood started to surface. The delicately balanced foundation of my marriage began to crumble under the strain.

We didn't have much money, nor did we have health insurance. Paying for extended professional help was a luxury we couldn't afford, so I was basically on my own, except for my brother who at that time was studying to become a therapist. We had long conversations about my frustrations and some about family issues, and he would often suggest books for me to read.

It was during that painful period in my life that he suggested that I write a fairy tale. He said to just start with "Once upon a time" and let the story unfold. He said I might be amazed at what it would evoke. The act of writing those four words and the experiences of recording the story that followed, became a turning point in my life and a powerful illustration of what lie dormant within me waiting to be tapped. It opened my door to the "kingdom within."

My varied studies exercised my mental muscles, helping me intellectually to learn to grasp complex and abstract ideas and to raise questions as different concepts challenged my belief systems. Writing became my way to explore those questions and integrate the answers.

There were often times as I walked through various belief systems that I felt like I was "relearning" something I already knew. I had a strong sense of "gathering" or "weaving" - of threads of ideas that would eventually give me a bigger picture. I was also intrigued by my unequivocal attraction to some material and total indifference to other material. What inside of me did the pulling? Why did some material resonate within me as "truth," only later as I discovered another "truth" to be discarded?

Once I started on this journey of exploration, I could not stop pondering, searching, gathering, or yearning anymore than I could stop breathing. Then two new dimensions were introduced to me in Psychosynthesis and Tarot.

I was taking an introductory correspondence course on the symbolism of the Tarot cards[1], (based on the Rider-Waite deck) at about the same time as I began to write the fairy tale. Incorporating the characters of the cards was a natural direction for me to go. The cards depict archetypal stages of the human journey, and once I began to work with them in an active way, they became profound guides to me.

Since I took that course over 20 years ago, I have studied several versions and interpretations. What I write about Tarot in the following story is a synthesis of what I have learned from the many outside sources as well as my own internal experiences working with them.

A spiritual direction retreat I attended based on Psychosynthesis[2] opened a powerful doorway to the inner landscapes of my psyche through the use of imagery.

Once I would start writing and interacting with an Archetype[3] in imagery, the story would take on a life of its own, becoming an otherworldly experience, a waking dream. By journaling as I explored, I was able to bring the experience of the journey back to the outer world. I discovered a rich and fascinating kingdom within my own psyche where deep and profound healing and growth could take place.

In tandem with, but separate from the fairy tale, were the emotions I grappled with. Those I found it easy to express in poetry. The next natural step was to weave the poetry into the story.

In order to expand on the tale more than I could if I stuck to a strictly fairy tale format, I found it useful to write a story within a story, which became a creative challenge in itself, but helped me to expand on what I learned considerably. I was realizing so much with this process that couldn't be written into the fairy tale, but I felt that the fairy tale needed to remain. Another layer had to be created and that is where Amethyst came in.

The format of the book is an illustration of how I was living and turning to my inner world for escape. The escaping saved my life by providing a vehicle to explore and release the pain of my reality which ultimately brought me back to a fuller and richer experience of life.

If there is importance in this work, its usefulness lies in the process it illustrates, as well as lessons learned. I had stumbled onto a practical way to synthesize everything I was learning, thus enabling me to create a powerful tool of self-discovery which became the vehicle for my own healing.

Eventually, other considerations began to present themselves, as I was able to look at my life from a more objective and clinical point of view. I began to play with the idea of "myth" which brought me to the realization that the "fairy tale" of "happily ever after" and the belief in that outcome is the stereotypical myth. Myth as Archetype is the journey of the soul through predictable stages. I realized that I started out writing a fairy tale looking for the happily ever after theme and ended up writing a mythical journey. I started with the expectation of the stereotype and arrived at the feet of the archetype.

Once I could see the difference between the fairy tale myth and the archetypal myth, I began to wonder if we were all living the same basic mythical blueprint (a story illustrating common archetypal influences and themes) and could we change the blueprint by becoming conscious of it, or do we even want to? By understanding the archetypal themes in our lives can we consciously harness the energies and use them in a creative manner? Using my life as a study, I set out in hopes of learning what I could about the above questions.

I had completed the story when I came across the book "The Emerald Tablet" by Dennis William Hauck, published in 1999. He describes the stages of the Alchemical Journey, and to my delight I was able to see those stages within the story I had written. This also served to affirm to me that I was indeed experiencing something larger than myself, a predictable pattern of development. I think those stages as outlined in this book constitute one complete turn on a never ending spiral of growth. It remains to be seen whether or not I can make a conscious difference in the way I experience subsequent stages during future trips around the spiral now that I have an understanding of the game plan. Whatever lies ahead, this is the story of how I arrived to this point.

An important concept that will present itself during a spiritual growth process is the concept of the "observer" or "witness," which is a way of stepping aside and viewing oneself and the events of one's life in an objective or neutral manner. When we see a movie, we are in a somewhat "witnessing" state. We may be pulled in emotionally to the story, but at the same time we are just observing the story.

I found it helpful to become such an observer to my own life. I was able to release attachments that formerly had kept me a prisoner and see my life as one story among many, with a pattern of recognizable stages. Once that happened, the issues lost their grip on me.

I have come to the conclusion that certain concepts in the collective unconscious are working their way through and into our consciousness. A new paradigm or way of thinking is laboring to be birthed into the world. I see it in the personal stories of contemporary writers exploring the terrains of their own psyches and in the revelations of some spiritual teachers. The concepts must come through the belief filters of each individual, but there seems to be some underlying messages.

I have been writing the notes and poems that constitute this story since the early 1980's. I didn't know where I was going with the story, or even how to end it, until I arrived at the end of the fairy tale.

I think the timing of finishing this book is relevant to the times we live in. For many who have tuned in to the development of the new paradigm and struggled to express personal impulses coming from its descent into this plane, I think you will identify with my experiences. For those who haven't tuned in yet, I hope my excursions may help you to sort out your own remnants from the fire and begin to see the new ships on the horizon.

Much of the power of story is its ability to touch some truth within the reader and bring it to consciousness. As you read the story, it is my hope that for you dear reader, the Essence of your truth will be triggered. As a beloved teacher used to say, "Let us speak to you between the words."

The setting for the tale is modern, "not far from now" as the opening sentence describes, and one of many excursions outside the "box" of expectation. A fairy tale can happen now just as much as it could happen in the 17th century, only now the castle has some modern conveniences, and the characters use cars and airplanes, not carriages and horses.

Robert Bly in "The Maiden King" which he wrote with Marion Woodman says that we are being asked to move from the psychological to the mythological stage or way of thinking. That statement encourages me that possibly by responding to my brother's suggestion, I unwittingly tapped into a deep impulse within the collective that was waiting to be given a voice.

Lark Ferguson, November 2001

PROLOGUE
AMETHYST'S DECISION

Amethyst and Hugh lived in a small two story home on the Northern California Coast. It sat back far enough from the shore to be sheltered from the inevitable storms that were a part of coast life and yet close enough to give them a breathtaking view of the ocean.

Amethyst loved the Northern Pacific Coast and had fulfilled a lifelong dream with the purchase of their home. Her favorite feature of the home was a long closed in sun room along the entire west end facing the ocean. It had windows that would open to allow the fresh sea air in on warm days and a wood burning fireplace for cozy warmth when the weather was cold and blustery.

"This is where I will write," she had exclaimed to Hugh when they looked at the house. "Look Sweets, there is room enough for my computer and built-in shelving to hold my journals and your notebooks and music books and still plenty of room for your keyboard and your computer! You know how I love to hear you play as I write. We will live in this room" she exclaimed excitedly!

Hugh grinned. He had never seen her look quite so excited, her eyes shining with anticipation. He could see that on this day there would be no turning back. This was to be their new home. They had waited a long time for this event, for they had decided years before to live by the sea for the remaining years of their lives.

Now retirement was just a few years away. These last working years had been spent looking for this special place they both dreamed of. Their dream was to spend their retirement years for the creative pursuits they had not had time for when they were both working full-time jobs. Both of them enjoyed excellent health, created by years of a tenacious adherence to a healthy and mutually supportive lifestyle.

The couple had built their relationship encouraging each other in the fulfillment of their individual dreams. It wasn't hard, for they each held a deep admiration and respect for the others' abilities. The time was coming when they could focus full time on their heart's work, and buying the house was a big start.

Upstairs, directly above the sun porch was a large spacious loft which made a perfect bedroom. It had huge windows facing the ocean and a fireplace which shared the same chimney as the sun room's fireplace. They both loved the radiant and cozy heat of burning wood.

It was in front of their bedroom window that Amethyst had placed her drawing board, and art supplies. She would live by the windows, using the changing moods of the ocean and landscape for her inspiration and her muse.

When the windows were open, the gentle roar of the surf was a soothing mantra to their ears, trickling through their bodies in calming waves of ecstasy and putting them in the most creative space they had ever experienced in their lives. At night that same mantra lulled them into deep restful sleep.

Amethyst was sitting in the sun room sipping on her morning coffee, enraptured by the view as she always was. The late morning sun had burned through the fog, promising a bright and sunny day ahead.

On this day she felt a strong impulse to drag out her old journals and poetry. They were moved in and settled, and now she could start on the project she had promised herself she would complete in this wonderful place.

It had been years since she had lived the story her journals told, and today the story held her interest in an unusually detached and yet intimately familiar way. It was like reading a letter from an old beloved friend she hadn't seen in years. She sat in her favorite rocking chair, watching the sun dance on the water and the tide play on the sandy beach and mused about where her life had taken her.

Here she was, sitting in her own writing room of her own little home by the sea living with her beloved. She was happy and had fulfilled dreams that had been years in the making.

She was also feeling a familiar tension within her, a sure sign to her that change was on the horizon. The feeling was pleasant, which assuaged the fleeting anxiety that usually accompanied these feelings. She knew without a doubt that she was on the verge of a breakthrough. She also knew that she had some unfinished business to complete before the breakthrough could happen.

Amethyst and Hugh were both Seekers. They had spent their lives looking for the deeper truths they felt spiritual teachings of the world held. It was actually seeking which had brought them together, and it was seeking that forged a strong bond between them.

She thought back to the years she spent with Lazaris[1], one of her first teachers. She had learned about a future self who could actually guide her along a chosen path to its fruition. All she had to do was allow herself to make contact with that future self and move in the directions of its promptings. She was taught to recognize these promptings as strong inner impulses or intuitive knowings, and she had gradually learned to respond to them.

She was at this moment in time realizing the culmination of dreams she had set in place years ago under Lazaris' guidance. She was an almost completed version of that Future Self. A chill of exhilaration went through her as she realized the full ramification of that thought. At the same time, she knew something was still missing. She had fulfilled the physical goals she had set for herself. The deeper, psychological yearnings were still in the process of unfolding, and she had one goal yet to be realized. That goal was to write the story of the journey she had taken, to keep the promise she had made to herself years ago. She had packed away her journals, knowing that the day would come when she would go through them and assemble the story they held.

Where to start? That was the musing on this clear day, the crisp ocean breeze kissing her face, feelings of utter contentment mixed with creative tension teasing her, reminding her that she would progress no further until she had fulfilled that long ago promise to herself.

Hugh walked into the sun room and sat down at his keyboard. Amethyst didn't acknowledge his presence as she usually did, she was lost in a world of her own.

"What is the matter, Sweets?" he said. "You look like your a million miles away."

"I am," she replied pulling herself out of her reverie. "I feel I am ready to start writing this story, but now that I am actually set up to write, I haven't a clue where to start!"

Hugh looked at her contemplatively for a few minutes. In his characteristically helpful but non-intrusive way he finally said "Tell me what you want to say. Maybe by verbalizing it, you will get a sense of how to get it started."

Amethyst looked at him somewhat shyly, verbalizing her ideas before she had formulated them was very hard for her. She liked to have her ideas firmly within her grasp before she ever shared them with anyone, even Hugh. She felt his love for her and his willingness to help by listening and grappled to explain the concepts she wanted to express.

"Your right," she said. "I appreciate your willingness to take the time to listen to me, to help me get started, so bear with me, and I"ll try to explain," she said with a reticent grin.

Amethyst took a deep breath and began. "There are schools of thought which teach that it is through the study of myth, legend and archetypes that we discover the unconscious forces that drive us. The stories come straight out of the collective and can give us some clues of how our consciousness works. Myths are stories of universal truths played out by archetypal or typical characters."

"You remember when I told you how my brother suggested during that very difficult time in my life that I write a fairy tale?" Hugh nodded. "Well, I think that is how I want to write the story. I started writing parts of a fairy tale when he suggested it. Now re-reading my notes and looking back over my life and the lives of the women I know, I realize that I have lived a life that is a variation on a general theme unique to my generation of women." We have experienced so many changes in the expectations of the way women are supposed to be in this world. There is a common thread, in that generational shift. I want to identify it, because I think the blueprint of my story comes from archetypal promptings common to my generation and is our myth or fairy tale.

"At the same time, I am fascinated by the archetypes especially as they are depicted in the Tarot cards. I see the hints of a process in the cards, and I think by writing the story I may discover the process."

"Hmm, as I say that it brings to mind several questions: If we are all living the same basic story illustrating common archetypal influences and themes which I see as a gender myth, could we change the myth by becoming conscious of it?"

Hugh mused, "That is a good question. I wonder if by becoming conscious of the mythical theme running through your collective lives, you would change the myth. Where do you see the archetypes fitting in?" he asked.

Amethyst sighed. "This is work, trying to figure this out, but I think that if we understand the archetypal influences in our lives, we can harness the energies and direct them in a creative way."

Hugh became more enthusiastic as he began to understand the possibilities of what she was trying to do. "It seems to me there is a great deal to be learned by writing and studying your personal myth. We both know that our generation is in the middle of a major paradigm shift. Look how much has been accomplished and changed just in the last few years, let alone our lifetimes thus far. Your approach to this process could be very enlightening! I can see the archetypal fairy tale idea as a great vehicle to explore your personal story turned myth."

"Now I am getting excited, Hugh!" Amethyst exclaimed. "That's it! I will use a fairy tale as the vehicle to tell the story. As I say that it brings to mind what I have heard Lazaris say so many times,'there is magic in the telling.' I hope I can unleash the magic that lives within the events by telling the story," she said wistfully.

"I think I will call the main character simply 'The Woman', because in the telling of the myth it becomes every woman's story to some extent," she mused.

"Try it that way and see how it works," Hugh suggested, as he turned to his beloved music. "You can always change it if you don't like it." Amethyst nodded, but didn't need to say more, Hugh had begun to play.

It is easy to lose sight of the fact that writers do not write to impart knowledge to others; rather, they write to inform themselves.

Judith Guest

AUGUST 31, 1997

SINGING THE FLESH BACK ON THE BONES OF MY SOUL-SELF

What repressed my SOUL SELF? What stripped Her of Her flesh and turned Her into a bag of bones and buried Her deep in the tomb of my unconscious?

What will put the flesh back on Her Old Bones and resurrect Her, freeing her Her from the dungeon of repression that holds Her prisoner?

Is this the task of one who wishes to be reborn? Is this the work of one who wishes to become transformed? Is this the labour of rebirth I hear so much about?

Even though She was stripped of Her flesh and buried, what kept Her memory alive enough that I know She exists?

It was the bones themselves, rattling around in the hidden layers of my senses, taunting me with remnants of emotional memories, keeping me in distress.

I begin by asking the questions about how she was stripped to the bone in the first place. What dried her out, took her voice, shriveled her heart and withered her feelings?

How can she get back her voice, open her heart, and fill her tissues with the juice of emotion so they once again delight in the dance of feeling?

Buried in the depths of the unconscious, a map is needed to travel the terrain. Will a fairy tale suffice? I was told it is a powerful tool for accessing those deep, dormant parts of myself. Can I entice the Unconscious to speak to me in the fairy tale and myth in my life's journey?

The following pages explore the questions as they tell the tale. If there is "Magick in the telling," what "magick" will I discover?

"Deep within your lost, current and future dreams, you can
find the stuff of magic.
You can find the keys that lift you from your current plateau
to new heights of success...Dream,
you will find your way."

Lazaris

Calcination

..."a natural process that takes place over time, as we are gradually assaulted and overcome by the trials and tribulations of life.
...Calcination is working with Fire to burn away mental constructs and reveal a person's true essence."

The Emerald Tablet
Dennis William Hauck

THE PLAINS OF REASON

Its inhabitants
Caught in the throes of a destructive drama
Puts into subjection
Its female side
Steers Itself into logic
Afraid to look in
Beating its female
Staying tough.

Playing their parts well
Perpetuating a lie
Fostering a continuous split
A comfortable niche
Upon which they can rely.

With a schizophrenic consciousness
This plane is manipulated and controlled
No love or concern
Only a "scientific eye"
Do not trust your feeling side
Only logic must decide.

Man
Symbolically-physically outside
Logic and intellect his chief prize
Taught not to cry
To hide his feeling side.

Woman
Symbolically physically inside
Passive, Nurturing
Intuition, her chief prize
Allowed to cry, show her feeling side
But shunned by masculine pride.

Like the gods of ancient Myths
Into this world they come
Donning their male and female roles
Hiding from themselves the other side.

Little knowing the drive
For wholeness
Is what draws them together
And as they unite
Physically
Emotionally
Spiritually
They slowly awaken
To the side they hide
And the mystery of the real union.

As the outer
Masculine Principle
Joins the inner
Feminine Principle
On the Bridge of Understanding
This holy union
Begat a new birth.

For each is all
Conscious \ Unconscious
Outside \ Inside
Active \ Passive
Logical \ Intuitive
Masculine \ Feminine

The task of this plane
Neither inner nor outer must reign
Integration will free the pain
Raising the consciousness of Humanity
Away from this insanity
A new age ushered in!

CHAPTER ONE

THE WOMAN-A FAIRY TALE

Happily Ever After-(Whatever That Meant)

Once upon a time in a land not far from Now, on the Plains of Reason there lived a young princess. Like all princesses in the kingdom she was expected to grow up and marry a handsome prince and "live happily ever after," (whatever that meant).

Now the princess as she was growing up had dreams of becoming a dancer. She would spend hours listening to music while visions of dances would come to life in her imagination. She would then work hard attempting to express with her body all that the music said to her. When she was lost in expressing what she felt from the music, she was in utter bliss.

The Grandmother Queen of the realm allowed her to take dancing lessons, more to develop grace than to fulfill a young girl's dreams. It was reasoned that the grace would help to attract a handsome prince, so the lessons were allowed. Her dreams of becoming a dancer weren't taken seriously, however, so she figured they were not important. After all, what does a young girl know about these things! She was continually reminded that the real goal of a princess was to grow up and marry a handsome prince and "live happily ever after" (whatever that meant).

In due course of time the handsome prince appeared, and feeling like this was what she was expected to do, she married him, and they set out to "live happily ever after" (whatever that meant).

Into this royal family were born 4 princesses and 2 princes, and the young princess had now transformed into a woman. The Woman busied herself with the joys of motherhood and worked very hard at "living happily ever after." She appeared to be doing well, and family and friends congratulated her on her well-ordered life.

1

AS the years went by, however, she became more and more unsettled by the "happily ever after" bit. It just didn't seem to be working, and she began to think something was dreadfully wrong with her. The fear that she was abnormal made worse the small, but persistent pain that gnawed at her insides as a deep, almost unreachable yearning for something that she could not define. She became sad, often irritable. It was hard to be patient and loving to her children, and she was often found weeping for "no reason at all."

A Wall of Despair had developed around her which worried and angered Handsome Prince. His Charming Princess was losing her charm, and he would lose face if they were not living "happily ever after." He provided a nice castle for her, what more did she want. His questions only confused her more, mixing the deep despair with guilt because she could not answer. She didn't understand it herself. In her feeble attempt to make some sense out of what was happening to her she tried to write her feelings down:

FEELINGS

So deep inside me
Why?
Do I want to be free
or cry?
It's sorta like pain
I'm tense
Tears fall like rain
It doesn't make sense

My retorts are sharp
That hurts too
I don't mean to harp
How can I be true
And to who?

I need to understand
Everything

2

Not sure what it will bring
If anything

Please
Don't reprimand this obsessive dream
Sometimes I laugh and sing
and dance
Thru this illusive trance
and cling
But it doesn't last long
Reminded by a thought
Or Song
A feeling

Something is wrong.

The body that longed to dance began to grow heavy in protest at being denied it's medium of expression. On the Plains of Reason bodies were to be used for having babies, keeping handsome princes happy, and service to the kingdom. For a woman to find enjoyment in her own body was considered outrageously self-centered and certainly not something a devoted wife and mother would indulge in! Only service, that was the "good and righteous purpose for a body."

Now in this kingdom, once a soul committed itself to a body, the only way out was through a long and painful process of self-destruction. Once the body had fulfilled its purpose according to the beliefs of the inhabitant, it would automatically begin the process.

While growing up, the princess longed to be a dancer, but the goal imposed on her by the kingdom was to "marry a handsome prince and live happily ever after." Remembering her dreams, in contrast to her current reality, The Woman felt she was failing miserably. The feelings of resignation became the catalyst initiating this process of self-destruction. Release seemed the only answer.

The sad and lonely woman wandered around forgotten parts of the castle heavy with the weight of failure. In an effort to get away from everyone, she trudged up several flights of stairs until she found herself at the door of an unknown room in a tower. She was drawn to this room before she realized where she was going. She vaguely remembered someone saying that she was to stay away from this part of the castle, but she didn't care what happened to her and opened the huge wooden door and went inside.

The room was an old study library once used by one of her ancestors. It contained shelves of ancient books and notebooks long ago abandoned by a "modern" world as irrelevant to everyday life.

In one corner was a large desk. In a drawer, she found writing paper and pens. Beside the desk was a small fireplace. It had an ancient rug in front of it with strange symbols woven into it. Across from the desk and by a small window was a large rocking chair. She could sit in the chair and look out over the kingdom, and no one could see her. She could sit at the desk and write all that was in her heart, and no one would ever know.

She was enchanted. Here was a place where she could come to sort out all that was troubling her. As she browsed through the books, she wondered if they could possibly hold the answers to some of the questions that were plaguing her!! She had found a place to retreat from the world that could not help her.

She resolved to return to this place as soon as she could again and explore her new found room of treasures. She needed to get back to the family before they discovered her absence and started asking questions, so she left her secret room pulling the door tight behind her. For the first time in a long time she felt hope.

The Tower

With a sense of purpose The Woman would hurry through her work and as soon as it was done, she would sneak off to the Tower and all the discoveries it held for her eager mind to absorb. She was being stimulated and as she began feeling better about herself, the process of self-destruction began to slow down. She had also found a place where she could bring her music and dance to her heart's content. The heaviness that she had accumulated began to disappear.

The prince was at first pleased at the changes in his princess. He attributed it to her finally coming to her senses and realizing her place and accepting it. She was happier and easier to get along with, and for awhile the castle was a more harmonious place.

As time went on, The Woman began spending more and more time in the Tower, and several times the prince arrived home in the evening to her absence in the living quarters of the castle. This surprised him, he expected her to be there when he came home!

It would irritate him when she begged him to spend more time with her and the children, but it also gave him secret pleasure to know she depended on him so much. He felt such a sense of power and importance, reminding her of how much time he was spending building the kingdom for "her and the children." Now here she was, going off and enjoying herself and not acting very interested in him anymore. The prince sensed trouble brewing.

One day instead of going off to do his work in the kingdom, he hid and waited to see where she went and followed her to the Tower. After she left, he went in the room and discovered what she was learning and read some of her writings. He was very angry when he discovered that not only was she spending time in a forbidden part of the castle, but she was spending that time reading and writing and other such useless activities. She was learning things that could take her away from him, and he did not like that at all!! What if she became smarter than he? The knowledge she was gaining was already making her more emotionally independent, and he feared he would lose control over her.

He confronted her, forbade her to go back to the room in the Tower telling her she must stop all this foolishness at once. Other women in the kingdom were happy to care for their husbands and children, without having to sneak off all the time, and she could be too!! He reminded her of all he "had provided for her" that she did not appreciate, and she felt very guilty. He shamed her for taking so much time away from the family to pursue her own selfish activities. He reminded her of all the work she was neglecting or could be doing.

At first The Woman overcome with guilt, worked very hard at being what the prince wanted her to be. In this kingdom a princess always did what her prince said.

For awhile, with the memory of all that she had learned still fresh in her mind, she had plenty to think about and was able to keep her spirits up as she toiled through her daily chores. Eventually though, the deep dark cloud of depression cast its ominous shadow over her again, and The Woman had to slip away to her refuge in the Tower.

She told herself she would just have to be more careful about the time she spent there and make sure that everything that was expected of her was finished before she went. She was so miserable. It was either that or the self-destruction process.

"How do I reconcile my life with what I am learning?" She asked herself half aloud. Sitting curled by the fire, she picked up her journal and wrote:

What Are Dreams For?

Something inside me
A still small voice
Persistently hinting at a mystery
Calls to me
A passionate ache
Longing for relief.

Frustration and I
Constant companions
Knowledge-eagerly gained
I long to share
But he won't listen

He doesn't care!

A slave to the culture that bore and bred him
Only one school of thought accepted here
Sad, gray, droopy, ghostlike vitality
Fit into your mold, don't waver
As I wash my dishes, to wash them again
Clean up today, only to clean up tomorrow
I long for a purpose to make sense to my toil

Anguish wells up inside me
Spilling over into tears of despair
As I sit in my chair
The crackling fire tries to cheer me
And yet I feel cold
Even the fire's cheerful glow
Cannot warm my soul.

Please understand my searching
Explain it to me
Open up the mysteries of my heart
Set me free!

What is the reason for my existence?
Why, oh why am I here?
What is truth? Does it matter?
Does anything really matter?

My awakened curiosity
Has opened small avenues of discovery
That seem to call to me, mocking me
Teasing the loneliness with false hope

I am given a taste of what I seek
Only to have it withdrawn
Like elusive ghosts,
Leaving me lonelier than before.

Lark Aleta Ferguson

I cannot speak my heart
For it would not be accepted
Nor understood
I am punished for my pain
The struggle is so hard
And I am so discouraged
What are dreams for?

The insanity of my life goes on
Can no one sense my turmoil
Seething under this calm veneer?
Is this a normal state?
Do any feel as I do?
How do I ease the ache?
Assuage the fear?
Where do I go from here?

CHAPTER TWO
THE OLD ONE AND THE TREASURE CHEST

One night after the children and the Prince had gone to bed, The Woman quietly slipped away to the Tower. She hadn't been able to sleep and felt a strong urge to visit her hideaway. She built a small fire in the fireplace, pulled her rocking chair up by the fire, and as she sat there warming herself and thinking, her eyes fell on a small chest sitting in a dark corner, almost hidden. She had been so engrossed in the books and her writings that she hadn't noticed the chest, or had it even been there? She was incredulous as she thought to herself that she didn't ever remember seeing it there before!

She went over to examine it, dusted it off and realized to her surprise that it wasn't locked. She carefully lifted the lid, wondering what she would find. It was a box of odds and ends, a small vase, a few statues, some old pictures, a gold ring shaped like a rose.

Toward the bottom of the chest, she discovered a rectangular package wrapped in purple velvet and tied with a faded gold ribbon. She carefully untied the ribbon and unwrapped the small package. It was a deck of cards, but unlike any she had ever seen. Each card had a figure on it with names like The Fool, The Empress, The High Priestess, The Lovers, and so on. She looked at each one of them, and as she did, she laid each one out on the rug by the fireplace. She was enchanted by the figures and the symbols on the cards.

One she was especially drawn to was a figure of an old man dressed in a gray hooded robe, standing on top of what seemed to be a mountain and holding a lantern in his hand. The name under the picture read "The Hermit." As she held it, she felt a strange vibration in her hand. The card began shaking so vigorously that it literally jumped out of her hand and fell to the floor. The figure in the card started to move, growing larger until standing before her was a life size bearded old man.

9

"Do not be afraid, my child," the Old One said in a comforting soft voice that put her instantly at ease. "Your questions, your searchings, your trips to this Tower all have been setting the resonance for the day I would come to you. You are ready. It is no accident that you found the chest tonight, for it is time. By coming to the Tower, you have opened up latent, important parts of yourself. Now that you have arrived at this juncture, once you give permission to continue you cannot turn back. You must go forward into the destiny you were born to fulfill."

"Already, you have discovered that you can find relief from your pain by writing your experiences down. This gift will continue to serve you well if you are willing, for your destiny involves this activity in a very intimate and profound way. Are you interested in hearing more?" he asked. The Woman could barely squeak out an answer, she was in such awe of what was happening, but she managed to whisper "yes, yes, please go on."

He smiled at her in a reassuring manner and continued to explain, "You see, you are from the ancestral lineage of the Story Tellers, who were healers and teachers. In ancient times they traveled from place to place telling stories, teaching lessons, helping people learn about new ways through the metaphor of story.

"Before you became a Story Teller, you spent a lifetime on Atlantis, and you were there at the time of its destruction. You were seduced by the power of your position at that time and participated in the experimentation that led to its destruction. You and many others have incarnated at this time when a similar kind of catastrophe is possible for the entire planet. You have collectively vowed that such a horrible event will not happen again.

"Dear one, you have traveled many lifetimes to come to this time in your planet's history. Through your work as a Healer and Story Teller, you have cleared a great deal of the guilt and karma you carried from your Atlantean lifetime, and you have progressed to the spiritual level where you have the potential for a complete awakening in this lifetime. However, in order to accomplish that goal, you also must

10

clear the familial issues of the life you are currently living, as these issues are part of your overall karmic pattern, and thus a component of the process of your complete awakening."

The Woman listened in raptured awe as the Old One spoke. He paused, and she said somewhat timidly, "kind sir, may I ask you a question?"

"Of course," he replied.

"What is the purpose of these cards, and why are they oddly familiar to me? I've never seen anything like them before, and yet I feel a sense of connection to them that I cannot explain."

The Old One chuckled and stroked his beard as his eyes met hers with a knowing gaze. As their eyes met, she felt a shiver run down her spine.

"The cards are familiar to you because of the life you spent as a Gypsy. In that life you used them for fortune telling, but you didn't grasp their deeper meaning nor use because it was not time for that information to be revealed to you," he explained.

"The cards you have before you are a picture map. They depict the stages of an incredible and mysterious journey which you have been on for many incarnations. Each card holds clues/lessons to the steps you need to take to find your way. Listen carefully, for I tell you a marvelous mystery.

"The pictures on these cards depict Archetypal Energies. Archetypal Energies are universal principles that affect everyone on earth, whether they know about them or not. As a way for you to become conscious of them, they will come to you in the form of inspiration, experiences, realizations, teachers, etc. and work with you directly. When you are not aware of them, they project events out into your world, and you become an unconscious, and often unwilling, participant. Obviously, if you are conscious of the projections and the manifestations of these Energies and learn the lessons, they no longer have power over you.

"You see, long long ago there was a time when knowledge of the journey depicted in the cards was at risk of being lost. Entities called Rememberers were appointed to perpetuate

11

the information of the Journey of Awakening to anyone who showed readiness. It was imparted from teacher to student and not written down anywhere.

"There came a time, during a very dark period in history, when even the Remembers were at risk of being lost to this plane of existence, and if they were lost, the information they held would go with them. In order to keep the information from being destroyed, for future generations, picture cards were created which told the story to anyone ready to discover it. To everyone else they were just picture cards, except for the Gypsies. Ah the Gypsies, rascals of intuition that they were!" he exclaimed. "The Gypsies sensed that the cards held a mysterious power and discovered that when they laid them out, the cards told a story which would manifest for the person for whom the story was being told. So you see, you have already developed a rapport with these energies from your Gypsy days."

"The Pilgrimage you have ahead of you will lead you to a deep understanding of these energies. By learning to work with them in the original way, you will help restore old knowledge and at the same time create a new map for the times you now live in.

"By the look on your face I think I have given you enough history for one night."

"You have given me a lot to ponder," said The Woman thoughtfully. "So how do I work with these energies now?"

"For now just study the cards. Your experiences will bring more information to you as you need it, and I will explain how to use them in a moment," he replied. "First there are some things you need to understand before you work further with these energies."

"Remember," he went on, "these energies will not dictate your journey, but will help you to glean the meaning from the experiences of your life and help you discover the direction you intended to go long before you were born into this life."

"It might help you to know that there are many like you who on their own have discovered the Tower" he went on to explain. "All of you must study in seclusion until you are strong and have become fairly clear of your karmic patterns. I, along with the Energies illustrated on the other cards, are to be your guides for now. As you continue on your journey and grow in spiritual understanding of your purpose, you will begin to attract many of these people to you, and eventually many stories will be told. I know you are unhappy on the Plains of Reason, but for now you must stay here and learn. Your present task is to learn how to straddle both your inner and outer worlds comfortably. Once that has been accomplished then you will be ready for the next phase in this Work. For now be busy with the tasks at hand and trust the process.

"To work with any of these Energies simply do as you did tonight, lay the cards out. One will take on a special attraction and will work with you in some way. It may be that you are taken on an inner or outer journey, or inspired to write a poem, or story, or a being will manifest as I did and teach you directly. Stay with each card until it loses its attraction to you, for then its lesson for that stage of your growth is complete.

"I will be watching over you, as I always have and will come to you when you need me. Look for me especially in times of transition. I am called The Hermit, the Way Shower, I carry the lantern of The Light of Understanding and shine it on your path with great love for you.

"Keep in mind that I and the other Guides from the cards can only help you if you ask, but once invoked, each has a job to do and the power to carry it out. Do not invoke us lightly. Come to us reverently and ask for guidance.

"This is your journey, you must make your own decisions, however, whatever choices you make, we are available to help you glean understanding and growth from the outcomes that you manifest.

Your path is arduous, but not an impossible one. Are you willing to continue?" he asked.

"Oh yes," she replied emphatically. "You are the answer to so many prayers. I am so excited to be hearing this. Please go on." she implored.

"Alright" he said. "Now, here are a few ideas to keep in mind:

"Each person you encounter on the path has a personal vision that he/she is trying to fulfill. Through the Law of Attraction your relationship with each one will help both of you to grow in some way toward the fulfillment of that vision. The relationship will not end until the reason you came together is fulfilled.

"Each person you meet and event you encounter is a mirror of something in you. To help you find the mirror ask yourself the question-What is in my belief system that brings this person/event into my reality at this time? If it is a person that you are attracted to, ask yourself what qualities are in this person. They are probably qualities you have and are unaware of. If you are repulsed by someone, they can be characteristics you refuse to see in yourself."

"Pay close attention to the dreams that you remember. Through them I will often send messages and instructions."

"In the course of your Journey, you will be allowed access to eleven Archetypes, not necessarily all of your own choosing. The number of cards is limited, and for the most part, the choice of what you draw will be yours, unless an archetype is invoked unconsciously because of a dilemma. If you need help and cannot seem to chose a card, turn the deck over, ask for guidance and draw. You will draw the card you need. It is in the intent of the drawing, the asking, that the help comes."

"We do not bring you this awareness of your destiny until you are ready and at a point in your evolution where your chances of succeeding are very high.

"I have a parting gift for you. Here is a blank book for you to record your process in and a pen. Both have magical qualities to them. They will help you bring the answers you seek to the surface of your consciousness. All you have to do is ask a question and wait. The answer will come, often in mysterious ways. Don't forget to record them."

"Congratulations dear one, for the work you have accomplished to bring you to this state of readiness. I'll be around."

With that the OLD ONE began to fade and slowly disappeared, and the card was just a card once more.

The Woman sat by the fire for a long time in disbelief and awe of what had just transpired, clutching the gifts from the Old One. She flipped through the blank pages of the book. They seemed to call to her. She fondled the pen.

"Tangible articles to prove to myself he was really here," she thought to herself, and felt a chill of excitement go through her. Finally, she reluctantly put the pen and book in the treasure chest to keep them safe, doused the fire, and left to go to bed. She was so excited about all that the Old One had told her that it was hard not to talk about this profound series of events that were happening to her.

She kept it all locked up in a safe place inside of her, however, and went about her life living for the times she could return to her Tower.

The Call

See the Mountain yonder?
The solitary figure at the top?
His lantern casts a light
Into my darkness
And I am left with nowhere to hide.
Now faced with a choice
forever bound to abide

Alone, a bridge I pass over
A point of no return
For I have crossed the Bridge of Decision
A pilgrim I've become.

From the outside I travel inward
Mustering all the courage I contain
Toward a path of peril and adventure
Of fire and wind and rain

The cold chills my bones
Tears freeze upon my face
T'is a journey I do not embark on lightly
For the I who starts the climb
Will vanish without a trace

The Figure holds the Light
He beckons to me from the top
I start the climb, a strange force compelling me
There is no way to stop

For I have crossed the Bridge of Decision
In answer to countless prayers
The Hermit has appeared to guide me
To the refuge beyond my tears
As on the Path His lantern sheds
The Light to reflect my fears.

From the Outside I travel Inward
A Pilgrim I've become
To the Self who dwells inside me
My journey Home has begun.

The Fool

After her first experience with the cards, and meeting the Old One, The Woman could hardly wait to get back to the Tower just to see what would happen next. It was so exciting to know she actually had a guide who could help her sort things out. Finally, she was able to get away, and off she ran to her Tower.

She took the cards from their hiding place in the treasure box and laid them out on the floor. She picked up her book and pen and laid them on the floor beside the cards. The one that attracted her attention on this cold, wintery afternoon was one called "The Fool." She picked it up, expecting the figure to come to life as The Hermit had done, but it did not.

The Woman sat by the fire for a long time, holding the card in her hand. She was intrigued by the picture of a young person standing happily at the edge of a cliff, a small dog as a companion. What could it possibly mean? Following the instructions of the Old One, she held the card and sat staring at it. She would look at the card for awhile, and then she would feel compelled to look at the fire.

After staring into the fire for quite some time, a figure seemed to be coming toward her through the flames. She watched it grow larger. He was a beautiful, horselike creature with a horn in the middle of his head. "A Unicorn of all things" she exclaimed to herself. He was white and sparkled with a radiance that emanated all the colors of the rainbow. He was magnificent! Remembering that she must have her book and pen in hand, once the adventure began, she grabbed them and wrote the following account of the adventure.

The Unicorn

A unicorn passed my way one day
And beckoned to me "come,
"Thru fantasy we'll laugh and play

17

Hurry love, its' fun!
"Your world of thought and feeling
As real you see as this
I am sent to you
By the Bearer of Light
To be your guide in flight
And as we travel
Adventures unravel
You'll long remember
The journey of this night."

Remembering the words of the Old One
I asked if his name be "Inspiration"
He narrowed his eyes
Looked straight into mine
And with a nod of his head he said
"Tis True and we have some plans for you
But you must decide if you'll ride
I'm only here to be your guide."

I sighed.
Even on an adventure I must decide.
"C'mon Inspiration," I cried.
"Show me the plan
I'll follow along the best I can!"
His eyes twinkled mysteriously
"Many things you will learn this night
Some will even cause you fright
Hang on with all your might
It will all be right."

"Let's go!" I said,
He tossed his head
And from the tower we plunged
Into a world devoid of time & space
a very special creating place
How
with a unicorn
does one keep pace?
A place of magic
Where worlds come into being
And sound is seen
As symbols and design
Dreams are experienced for the feeling
Thought takes form and lives
And flowers bloomed before my eyes
And I felt their sighs.
All languages were heard as one
And I saw myself take form
From my desire
To live the dreams I create
A cosmic dance
A merry trance
Varieties of fate.

Bewildered and in awe
Of all that I saw
Engrossed in thought
I pondered my fate
And found myself at a gate
To the Temple of Life
I'd been brought.

In the presence of a Cosmic Master
My heart began to beat faster
And I began to quake
As His voice boomed out
"So you have discovered the Tower
And been presented to the Essence of Power.

Lark Aleta Ferguson

*The Old One told me you'd come
On the back of Inspiration!
From the Plains of Reason
To sojourn with us for a season."*

*"Do you seek knowledge of the Inner World?"
He asked
"You have set before you quite a task,
For you will be required to integrate
Into the world of time and space
All that you may perceive
From the understanding you receive
In the Timeless Realm."*

*"Once your task is complete
The wholeness you seek
Will be your reward
For you will understand your origins
From the Timeless Realm
Where dreams are born
To be played out in the world of time and space
That very unique learning place
Across the Plains of Reason
Through the Valley of Experience
Along the Path of Discovery
As it winds its way up the Mountain of Enlightenment."*

*A Tapestry of Illusion woven
On the Loom of Polarity
Using the threads of
Sun and Moon
Light and Shadow
Joy and Sorrow
Cynicism and Hope
The Mountain and the Abyss
the Sword and the Cup
The Oasis and the Mirage
Will be hung in the Archives of Existence
Upon completion of your journey*

20

As a remembrance of accomplished deeds
On the Plains of Reason.

NOW As The Fool Alone I stand
on the Precipice of Illusion
Equipt with the Loom of Polarity
Aware of my fate
I pass through the final gate
Afraid to go
Eager to start
This Journey to my Spiritual Heart.

Again Inspiration appears
And I climb on his back
So much has happened
I can't keep track
In less than a minute
I'm hurling through space
To the place
Where time meets it once again.

As I approached the junction
My mind began to function
flooding my awareness with full blown realizations
of the many dimensions existing within me
And I approached the Tower
Full of a new Power
Knowing I would keep on
Writing this incredible song!
From this Vortex of Realizations
Threads of understanding appear
To be woven onto the Loom
The picture becomes clear!

OUT OF THE MANY DIMENSIONS OF MY BEING
I AM
A unique expression of the life force that created me.

I AM AT TIMES A CHILD
Playing, running free
Wind at my face
Laughing with glee
Loving, giving, laughing, living
Throwing tantrums, demanding, forgiving.
Ecstatically alive
Seeing the world thru fresh eyes
Feeling hurt by shallow lies.

I AM A WOMAN
In biological expression of human form
Part of a sisterhood of immense responsibility
Matrixes of Spirit's seed
Gateways of manifestation
Sensitive to emotional need
In service to life we are forced to bleed
Expected to nurture
Intuitive by nature
Brimming with possibility our hearts yearn to express.

I AM PART MAN
Please understand that presumption
I sense an essence that makes that assumption
An energy dwells inside me
And with his penetrative focus
Does what he can to guide me
I fulfill his need
In my desire to succeed
A sense of adventure fills me with tension
A world awaits my invention.

I AM A MOTHER
Incredulous
As I've grown and watched emerge from me
Each precious infant
Felt it suckle at my breast
Tugging at feelings
From the deepest part of me
In awe of my own vitality
That can bring into physical form
A fresh new life
To love, nurture, enjoy
And watch grow
And be a part of me
And yet so "other"
And I love and treasure
And sometimes resent
Being a Mother.

I AM A WRITER
A heart full of emotion
Feelings, thoughts, a virtual ocean
How I struggle
To pour out the sea of thought
that is my mind
on flat paper!

I AM AN ARTIST
Driven by visions in my head
Longing to be on canvas spread
Calling to my willing, but untrained hands
to capture the richness I see
To give it form
Allow it to be.

I AM A GARDNER
Planting the seeds of desire
In the fertile garden of my imagination
Watering it from the great sea

Of passionate creation
Tending flowers from my heart
Watching them blossom
In the events I start.

I AM A LOVER
Full of feeling and desire
In search of the "Other"
Who will set me on fire
And transform me
And complete me
And set me free
To grasp the mystery.

I AM A DREAMER
Struggling in this bondage of illusion
Yearning for the music
That transports me into enchanted lands
Of pastoral scenes and extravagant feelings
Reminding me of the limitlessness of possibilities
In the landscape of my mind
a vagabond at heart
Searching for a place to start.

I AM A SEEKER
Exploring the world of time and space
Traveling toward the horizon of grace

I AM A SCHOLAR
Searching for knowledge
In the Archives of Existence
The journey is my college

I AM A MYSTIC
Seeking union
In quest of the key
That unlocks the door to me.

I AM

A philosopher, a dreamer
A lover, a schemer
A parent, a child
Usually tame, sometimes wild
I have a shadow side
I can't always hide
Nor do I want to

I AM THE FOOL
Standing on the Brink of Discovery
Jumping off into unknowns
So caught in the drama of the illusions
That seem so real
I often catch myself believing them.
I seek, explore, discover, love, laugh, cry
Feeling at times desolate and lonely
Often full of joy and hope
As I travel through the mountains and valleys
Of my life's landscape
Learning more of who I am.

CHAPTER THREE

SHIVA DANCES

The Woman's brother came for a visit. It was always an event for her when he did, because he was someone she could talk to who understood her. He had had his own problems with the "happily ever after" bit and found his sister to be someone he could confide in about what troubled him. She had shared the Tower with him, and he encouraged her to continue visiting it. He even brought her books that she could keep in the Tower.

This visit her brother told her about a meeting where many authors and thinkers of a new way would be and asked her if she would like to go with him. The Woman had become less and less communicative with her husband, as she withdrew more and more into the world which was captivating her. The Prince thought maybe a trip away from the castle would do her good. He was also feeling somewhat guilty because he realized he had been a little harsh with her. After all, in his own way he loved her and wanted to see her smiling. So it was decided that she would go with her brother to the gathering.

The Woman was very excited about the upcoming trip. Little did she know how much this event would change her life. It was here that she would meet Ben.

Before she left, she had wondered if the cards would foretell anything about the trip. She went to the Tower, and instead of looking at the cards, she put them in a pile so that she could not see what she would draw and reached in and pulled out THE LOVERS. As she held the card, a cold chill shivered through her body. She remembered what the Old One had said about the cards working in many ways. She was learning about the meanings of the cards, and she remembered that The Lovers often meant choice or a shift in direction. She was filled with a strong sense that this trip was important.

She was not attracted to Ben at first, he seemed so arrogant and sure of himself, but what he had to say piqued her curiosity, and she was drawn to him in spite of herself. Something seemed strangely familiar about him. After the meeting was over, just before they were to leave she introduced herself.

It was a beautiful early summer evening, the sun was just beginning to set on the occasion as they stood and talked like old friends. She learned that Ben was a traveler and teacher, and he seemed to hold before her all she could ever hope to learn. Before they parted, she consented to set up some classes where she lived.

After the trip, The Woman returned home with a renewed sense of purpose and informed The Prince that she would openly study and learn. He realized that she was right. He didn't have the right to limit her so much, even if she was his wife and he thought he could tell her what to do.

He resented the interests she had, but enjoyed her company more because she was happier.

Soon, Ben became a frequent visitor in their home, and a deep friendship grew between them. The Woman became more open about what she was learning, and others in the kingdom knew too, because Ben was teaching them as well.

Ben represented a world that The Woman longed to explore. He had studied about Egypt and visited there many times and was a reservoir of knowledge about ancient Egyptian teachings. He spent hours telling her stories of his experiences and discoveries, awakening something deep and ancient within her, filling her with yearning to be a part of the world he described. They began to speculate that they had spent time together in other lifetimes and strongly felt that they had first met on Atlantis. Ben suggested that they had served as Priest and Priestess in Egypt as well. It was on the level of ancient memories and spiritual seeking that their love grew.

They cherished the friendship that grew between them and for that reason made the decision not to become lovers. The Woman had a large family to raise, and Ben needed to be free to travel and teach. They knew a romantic entanglement would ruin the friendship, as well as her marriage. They talked of their love for each other and knew it would always be there. They both felt, however, that the Spiritual Work that they would do together was the reason they were brought together, and to that end they focused the friendship.

Ben, laboring under the guilt he felt over the destruction of Atlantis had taken a vow of poverty and service for this lifetime. He was an active facilitator of the Great Awakening which was happening all over the planet. His life was devoted to bringing back the lost knowledge from Egypt and Atlantis into this crucial time on the planet.

The Woman and her husband were growing farther and farther apart, as their interests took them in opposite directions. The Woman found deep satisfaction in delving into ancient teachings and applying what she learned to heal her present life as she had been instructed to do by The Old One. To her, the information she was discovering was a priceless treasure, a calling forth of ancient memories.

The Prince was busy with the affairs of his kingdom and making a fortune. He thought that her studies and interests were frivolous and held little relevance for their lives. He resented the time he believed she wasted on her pursuits, but humored her because she was the mother of his children, and he didn't want to have to deal with the everyday issues of raising a family. He put up with her "crazy notions" a long as she kept the castle clean, cooked the meals, tended the children and fulfilled her "wifely duties" to him. They were both devoted to their children, but communicated very little about anything else. The Woman became more torn between her growing love for Ben and her commitment to her marriage vows and love for her children.

On the surface The Woman appeared to be handling her love for Ben. In the Tower, however, where she could express what was happening her feelings told another story.

To Ben

I feel a tenderness toward you
that has become a meditation
thoughts of you
force deep contemplation

As mornings bring a new day
often, you come to play
in the corners of my mind

And I, wonderingly
Ah, bittersweet
mentally retreat
To thoughts of you.

Is it possible that you
could be thinking of me too?

I feel such a strong affinity
as our eyes meet
and we politely greet
each other.

Do you ever want to hold me
As I do you?
I ponder what is happening
and why?
Is it really true that events
"can be planned from the start"
that people can live in each other's hearts
and be drawn to each other?

And
Why does the world blend into nothing but you
when we speak
And it's so hard when you leave
Oh, how I wish you could stay!

Beloved, exquisite expression of God
So marvelously unique
How can I retreat from you
From this friendship
I'm compelled to seek?

Do you sense this, my friend,
And should it end?
And if it continues
What song of joy or sorrow
will be sung?

Several years went by, Ben visiting often as he passed through, or when he was scheduled to teach. The Woman continued to hide from Ben and the world the deep feelings she felt for him.

Eventually, the inevitable happened. Ben brought a guest with him and introduced her as the woman that he would be marrying. He announced that after their marriage they would be moving far away, and he wouldn't be teaching in that area any longer.

The news was devastating for The Woman. She knew Ben needed a companion, she knew it could not be her, she would not leave her family, and she realized that she loved him more than any man she had ever known. She had learned so much from him, and what she was learning had become her life. She knew that she needed to be able to share it, to work with it, and to be it. Ben had been a catalyst to that, and now Ben would be there no longer. Her pain was unbearable. She plunged into the grief she could not suppress. She was growing, she was feeling emotions she had never felt before, her life was full. Now, overcome with loss, she fled to the Tower looking for solace and for a place to hide and grieve.

Remembering And Trying To Forget

Like a poignant dream
On a warm summer's eve
Two people were drawn together
Our eyes met
In silent recognition
While the rays of the sun
Blessed our meeting
With a pyramid of light

Immediate captives
Of the force that brought us together
Only a look a handshake
Yet instant compatibility
Little did I know
What our innocent idealism would bring
As you touched me

This "chance" meeting
Of universal design
brought naive innocence
to the altar of idealism
breaking a sacrificial heart

Fleeting moments -so soon past
It isn't fair -they couldn't last
A taste of what I wanted, and needed
As I loved you

I try to be glad
For the short time we had
and grateful for all I learned from you
But your memory keeps my feelings so alive
They seem to have a life of their own
And I can't stop longing to see you again
I miss you so dear friend!

Overcome by grief and pain
I need to talk to someone
yet there is nothing to gain
Emotion tearing at my gut
A cord of attachment being cut

Crying till I'm spent
A new thought torments
A fresh burst of anguish
What comfort can cause it to relent?
A chasm of infinite grief
engulfs my thoughts and feelings
I grope blindly in an emotional darkness
Where is the light that will illuminate my path?

Show me
Where to look
How to look
What to look for
I really do not know and I need it so!

Aimless days stretch ahead of me
My heart is torn and aching
I don't understand
I dread going on
With endless nothing moments to fill my days
Surely all this could not have been in vain!

The Woman sobbed and sobbed as she realized how deeply she had allowed herself to be pulled into this emotional entanglement that she had no idea how to handle. She felt betrayed. She was doing what she had been taught was "right" staying with her husband and her children. She could not fathom living without her children, and she couldn't take them away from their father. What purpose did this pain serve? How did she get herself so deeply pulled into this. She had never in her life felt such pain engulf her whole being.

Her tears spent, she thought of the cards. "I so want to talk to the Old One, maybe he can give me some help, some way of understanding this," she said to herself.

She took the cards from their hiding place in the treasure chest and slowly unwrapped them. She looked through them, until she found "The Hermit." She held it, as she had done before and soon "The Old One" began to stir and take form in front of her.

"I needed to talk to someone, and you were the only one who I felt I could confide in. I hurt so much and miss him so much, I don't think I can endure this life or this marriage anymore! All I see ahead of me is emptiness. I thought I could do it, and when he was visiting and we could share and be together, it was enough. But now, he is truly gone out of my life, and I am sure I don't know what to do!" The Woman said weeping again as the words wrenched another wave of emotion through her.

"I know this is very difficult for you. It will be some time before you will be able to understand completely the role that Ben has played in your life. Suffice it to say that it was and is an important part, and your suffering will not be in vain, although it seems so now. Remember me telling you that you had much to learn in the Tower. There is a bigger picture being worked out here, and you play a part in it. Your experiences are preparing you for many things, take heart. You will see Ben again. Remember, he has devoted his life to a specific work and taking on a woman with a large family would divert him too much from the work he came to accomplish. You too have a work to do that will take you in directions of your own. It is hard to be in human form and see the bigger picture. Love complicates matters in countless ways. Trust what I say to you, my dear. You attracted the experience of Ben for many reasons which you will one day understand."

"Soon you will be ready to explore the impact he has had on you. All you are able to do at this time is feel your emotions. That is ok. It is part of the process of integrating the impact of Ben into your life.

"Remember when you drew THE LOVERS card, before your trip where you met Ben? The work of that Archetype is very powerful, changing those who come under its guidance in profound ways. It was no accident that you drew the card, however, by doing so you set an unalterable course. Think about that."

With those words, he disappeared, and The Woman was alone again in the Tower holding the card in her hand.

The only words that The Woman really heard were "You will see Ben again." They gave her a small amount of solace and a glimmer of hope. It was that hope that kept her going as the long empty days and months stretched ahead of her. Ben lived in her heart, and she knew that he always would.

In the aftermath of Ben, The Woman learned that her husband had been having an affair for quite some time. It was very hard news for her to hear, and although in many ways she was not surprised, the news was devastating to her. She had given up Ben to keep her family together, and now for what reason!! She was surprised at how hurt and angry she was at The Prince when she learned the news. He was the father of her children, and yet she could not communicate with him on any level but the the most mundane husband and wife level. He would not allow it. They had six children to raise who needed both a father and a mother.

The Prince said he wanted to keep the family together. He assured her that the affair wasn't about the two of them, and he still wanted his family. He promised her the affair was over, and that she needed to forgive and forget. They still had their family and could work things out. He also admitted that he had felt he was losing her to Ben.

She felt guilty because of her feelings for Ben and told herself she deserved this turn of events. She had remained physically faithful to her marriage vows, but she had not been emotionally faithful. She made the decision to stay in the marriage, "for the children's sake" and made a pretense of forgiving and forgetting, however inside she was seething with hurt and confusion. The marriage was now deeply damaged by the loss of trust which kept them both in an emotional standoff to each other.

A deep hole of yearning was left in her heart where Ben had lived, and her marriage felt cold and empty. Desolate and vulnerable, The Woman was drawn into another round of Shiva's dance.

Making Love

Making Love is
Waking, knowing
Today
I'll see you again.

Making Love is
Seeing your face
Your smile of recognition
(I wonder what your thinking)
Is our reunion hug and kiss
And starting a conversation
Before we even sit down
Because we have so much to say
It can't wait another minute!!

Making Love is
Sitting across the table from you
Locked in a trance
Where all I see is your face
And all I hear is your voice
And I become increasingly captivated by your presence
Until the rest of the world is only a blur
Suspended as we are
In a timeless world of our own.

Making Love is
Discovering each other's thoughts, feelings, views
Is loving the way you look
And feeling safe by the quiet strength you emanate
Is being intrigued by your maleness
And the feelings you arouse in me
Is being captivated by the sound of your voice
Reading the messages in your eyes
And your expressions

Making Love is

Touching, holding hands
Sharing a drink and toast together
Lost in the music
That will become forever our own.

Making Love is
Being carried away by a dizzying kiss
Into a frenzy of passion
Leaving me weak, and yet so charged
I'm energized for days after I see you.

Making Love is
Knowing you exist
Feeling blessed by our friendship

Making Love is
The gift of you and me and the miracle
Of realizing that in our separateness, uniqueness, aloneness
Two such beings can strike a common chord.

Making Love is
Bittersweet
Is life/death
Is frightening/fearless
Is resistance/surrender
Is timeless/fleeting
Is human/divine
Is you/me.

Making Love is
Pondering these things
Oft in the wee hours of the morn
When not able to sleep
I think of you
Savoring the memories and feelings
That gently haunt my head and heart.

Making Love
Is you, Is me

Is taking responsibility for ourselves
By taking the time to be together
To nourish each other
For the experience of relationship accelerates growth
And the one that Makes Love
Is a divine gift from the universe
A wondrous course of intense development
To be cherished and treasured
Bringing us another step closer to
Knowing and understanding Divinity
And the Ultimate Union.

CHAPTER FOUR

THE JOURNEY INTO NIGHT

Lord Sumina entered The Woman's life through Ben. He had been interested in Ben's work, and the two of them became acquainted during the time they both were working with Ben. Quite awhile after Ben left, Lord Sumina called her one day to tell her about a project he was working on that he thought might interest her. It had been a long time since they had seen each other, and The Woman thought it might be fun to see him again. They made arrangements to meet for lunch and discuss the project in more detail. The Woman was interested in what he was doing and said she would be glad to help him with it.

They worked together over several months. When they spent time together, The Woman saw her own vision, with many of its hopes and dreams mirrored in him. He had an air about him that fascinated and charmed her, and she found herself looking forward with much anticipation to their meetings.

Sitting across the table from him on one particularly cold, winter's day, laughing and talking and working as usual, she felt her mind drift into a reverie

Reverie

My friend, sitting here
Basking in the warmth of our friendship
Surrounding us in a cozy, loving bubble
I forget how cold it is outside

As we talk and laugh
And feel the easy natural chemistry between us
I am filled with a longing to touch you, to hold you, to kiss you
To feel your body against mine

39

And for a few timeless moments become one.

This desire I feel,
I wonder
Do you feel it too?
If I could read your mind
What would it reveal?

When they had finished with their work session and were preparing to leave, he hugged her as he often did, only this time he kissed her, so very tenderly, and they both knew knew that this friendship was becoming very special to both of them.

It was not long after that meeting that they became lovers. Lord Sumina became an important part of The Woman's life. He shared her vision, her interests, he was everything to her. She had found an outlet for all the love she could not express to Ben and was unable to give to her husband. He had captivated her heart and her imagination.

For the first time in her life she was physically involved with a man that she felt emotionally and spiritually connected to. She was fascinated with him, seeing him as her mirror image, the personification of the man that lived inside of her.

Lord Sumina traveled often, and his travels kept him away for long periods of time. When he returned and they were together, she was her happiest. The force of her love for him was having a very profound effect on her. She felt so alive, with a whole new kind of energy awakening within her, giving her confidence, helping her to become more aware of her own uniqueness and creativity. He encouraged her to develop her artistic abilities and to believe in herself. With his influence in her life she didn't need a special pen or book, or guide. She now experienced life through the fullness of her love for him, and within that richness she wrote. He brought her to life, and even though they had obstacles to overcome, she was beginning to feel that they would be able to work them out together. She felt she had finally found her soulmate, the one she was born to find.

The situation put her at a crossroads, and she knew some decisions were on the horizon. She had some thinking to do, and she needed some solitude in which to to do it, away from both Lord Sumina and The Prince and the world she lived in. The Tower wasn't enough this time. She needed to get far away.

The Woman made the decision to go to California for two months to take more training for her work. It would be during the summer, so that her second eldest child, Cherie could help the Prince care for the younger children. Their oldest daughter had left home the year before. The family held a meeting. Cherie had the chance to go on a trip with one of her friends, so they made arrangements for Cherie to take a trip of her own for several weeks arriving home a few days after her mother left. The Prince would stay with the younger children until Cherie arrived back at the castle and could take over.

The Woman had created a thriving business out of the castle, and she convinced her husband that the increased training would help her in her work, making it possible for her to add to the kingdom's fortune.

She also had another agenda. She wanted to see how The Prince and the children did without her, and she needed to feel what it would be like to be separated from her children and The Prince. She was "testing the water" for the decisions that inevitably lay ahead. They had made the mutual decision to stay together, but The Woman did not trust The Prince, and she was not convinced he would stay with her and the children. She was also unsure how long she could stay with him, and she was certain he was not the man she would grow old with. She knew that she would need to be able to take care of herself and the children better financially when the inevitable happened.

She loved Lord Sumina but along with those feelings was also a deep fear of losing him. She had felt the bitter sting of betrayal and loss, and that sting loomed on the edge of the rainbow she had around the two of them. Of those feelings she wrote:

Forebodings

Out of nowhere in time and space
you called I answered unaware
Until it was too late
Of the feelings that would follow
They just happened
And a dead part of me
(or I thought it so)
Began to stir

I fear it is too good to be true
To feel alive because of you
Like a moth to a flame
I am drawn to you
consumed by the fire
ignited in me
Transformed in the process
How do I say good-bye? Must I?

At times, feeling blue
when I don't hear from you
Hurt by the silence
tired of the pain
I become angry at the universe
for taunting me again

I was living getting by
I should have known better, I guess
So whimsical the feeling happiness
Must I once again close the door to my heart?
(To have left it shut would have been smart)

And yet -
You touched me I grew
You became my friend I blossomed
You made love to me
I became one with parts of myself

To that time unknown

In our brief, intense encounters
We've shared so much
It is not possible we won't keep in touch
I love you so dear friend.

The ominous dread The Woman felt was in fact a precognition as Fate was soon to deal a devastating blow.

It was in this state of ambivalence and trepidation that The Woman packed her belongings for a two month stay, hugged and kissed her children and The Prince and drove away heading the car west for the long drive to California.

The Uninvited

The Woman loved what she was learning, and she loved living by the sea. The cottage where she stayed was only a block from the beach. She would rise early every morning and take a long walk on the beach before class. In the evenings, she often would make a meal and take it to her favorite spot on the beach, where she would watch the sun go down, reveling in the breathtaking kaleidoscope of color the sea and sun painted each evening. The ocean air was exhilarating to her, and her sleep was deep and rejuvenating. She was content. Her life on the Plains of Reason seemed remote and almost unreal, and although she missed her children, she didn't miss her life there. She wanted to live forever near the ocean and hung onto each day, savoring it as long as she could.

The classes were divided into three day sessions. This particular day was the last day of a deeply probing session which had filled her with a feeling of aliveness and expanded energy unlike anything she had ever experienced in the past.

Then quite unexpectedly, about five in the evening she suddenly felt as if the life had been knocked out of her, and she felt a deep wave of sadness flood through her entire body. A terrible black feeling filled her completely, She drove back to her cottage as though she were in a trance.

She had only been in her room a few minutes when the phone rang. It was the Prince.

"Are you sitting down?" he said.

"No, why" she answered, and her heart started pounding.

"You need to sit down and take a deep breath," he said, stalling, trying to prepare her. She felt a cold shiver go through her, and she began to tremble.

"What is it?" she said impatiently into the phone.

"It is one of the kids," he replied.

"Which one?" she asked. There was a long pause.

"There was a car wreck. It's Cherie. She's in the hospital. She's not expected to live."

Not wanting to hear the full ramification of what he was saying, she said "Is she alive?"

"She is alive, but she is not expected to live through the night. I want you to think of everything you ever wanted to say to her. I am going back to the hospital as soon as I hang up here. I had to get the kids to your mother's. I will call you back and put the phone to her ear and let you talk to her. She is unconscious, but it may be your only chance to talk to her. I'll call you back within about 15 minutes."

"Alright" she said distantly, and they hung up.

The Woman sat in stunned disbelief and panic. She was so far away, and she didn't want to be living this. Not this. Every fiber of her being cried No! She sat in a numbed, trapped paralysis waiting for the phone to ring again. In what seemed like an interminably long time The Prince called back. He put the phone to Cherie's ear, as he said he would, and The Woman poured out her heart to her unconscious daughter, begging her to hang on, to get well.

The Prince came back on the phone and explained to his wife that the car she was riding in with some friends had overturned on a gravel road, and she had been thrown from the car. As the car had turned over it had landed where she was sitting, causing a severe blow to her head, and then turned right side up, throwing her out as it had turned. He said that the doctor had said that if she did live, it was fairly certain she would remain in a coma.

"What shall I do?" The Woman asked, "I still have about ten days before I am finished, my car is here, all my things" her voice trailed off. The Prince said "Please get a flight out as soon as you can and come home. We will deal with your car and things later. We need you to be here now."

"Alright," The Woman said reluctantly. In her initial state of shock and denial she somehow thought if she went on like she was, everything would be alright.

"Call me when you find out when your flight will arrive," he said pulling her out of her stupor of denial.

"OK" she said and hung up the phone. She found a phone book and as she was looking for the phone number to the airport, the phone rang again. It was her brother.

"I just heard about Cherie. Do everything you can fast before the reality of what has happened hits you," he advised. "Your in a state of shock right now, which is a good thing because it will keep you together enough to make arrangements."

"OK" she said obediently. She hung up, called the airline, booked the first early morning flight out, called the Prince back and told him when she would be in. Then she packed some things to take back and boxed up the rest of her belongings and piled them neatly in a corner of the room. She left a note to the owner of the apartment, called the school and left a message for her instructor, put her things in the car and drove to the airport where she spent what was left of the night. She did not want to receive a phone call that her child had died, she didn't want to talk to anyone or know until she arrived home the next afternoon what had happened. She wandered aimlessly around the airport the rest of the night until it was time for her to board the plane.

The Prince met her plane. His face was ashen, his news was that Cherie was still alive, but in a coma. The injuries were to her brain, and she had some bruises but other than that they didn't think anything was broken. They drove straight to the hospital.

The Woman's throat felt constricted as she approached the room where her daughter lay. As she walked into the room, her heart skipped a beat, and she gasped. She looked at her daughter in disbelief. She looked so peaceful, like she was sleeping. She surely didn't look like someone who was going to die! When The Woman spoke to her daughter, the vital signs on the monitor responded to her presence. The nurse said Cherie knew her mother was there. The Woman took the hand of her beautiful daughter and sat with her for a long time, talking to her, stroking her hand trying to grasp what was happening. Cherie lay peacefully, except for the occasional movements the nurse called "posturing." She had some bruises on her neck, and her lip was a little swollen, but other than that did not look injured at all.

Soon the doctor came in and asked her to step into a small room off Cherie's room to talk for a minute. He explained that the blow had injured her brain stem cutting off communication from that vital part of her brain to the rest of her body, and she would not ever regain consciousness. The Woman only able to take what was happening a minute at a time, asked him if she would live through the night.

"She may live through the night but" then he stopped, realizing she could not comprehend any more than that at the moment.

The Woman hadn't seen the younger children in six weeks, so toward evening she left the hospital to go to them. She had only been at her mother's for a few minutes when the hospital called and said they needed to get back as soon as possible. Cherie had stopped breathing and was put on a respirator.

And so it was that the long night vigil began. The family gathered around her, praying and drawing strength from each other. About three in the morning, the atmosphere in the room changed. It seemed brighter somehow. and a peacefulness settled on all the people in the room. The peaceful brightness lasted for about an hour and then changed again. At that time, Sunny, Cherie's younger sister and next to her in age said "That's it, she's gone" and got up

46

and went in to another room where there was a cot and went to sleep. She had not left her sister's side since she had arrived at the hospital after the accident the night before.

Later in the morning the doctors said that the tests they had run showed that she was brain dead, and all that was keeping her alive was the respirator. The agonizing decision was made to turn off the respirator and around 11:00 am that morning after the family had said their good-byes, Cherie's gentle and soft heart slowed down and stopped, and a bright light went out of the family forever.

It was a hot, humid and windy August day when the accident happened. The days ahead, as they like zombies, went through the ritual of burial and good-byes were just as unrelenting. It was as though even the earth protested the untimely passing of this fresh breath of spring that Cherie was. Cherie was a tall, blonde, radiantly beautiful, gentle 17 year old. She was loved by everyone who knew her.

The Woman wept as she remembered that the last time she saw her daughter was when the family took her to the bus. She had looked so radiant and happy that day as she embarked on what would be her only adventure. She was glad Cherie had been able to have that experience, but now they would never get to talk about it. She felt so terrible about being gone.

"What have I done, what have I done" she sobbed to herself over and over as she relived the events of the summer and thought of the wretched turn their lives had taken.

In the aftermath of this soul-wrenching ordeal, Lord Sumina, partly out of guilt and partly out of hopelessness for the situation, told The Woman he felt it would be better if they didn't see each other any more. He explained that he had hoped that sometime in the future they would be together. Now that this painful event had occurred he would not be a part of causing anymore pain to her family by splitting it up further. He could see no future for them and thought it would be easier if they both moved on and didn't communicate anymore.

Easy for him, he traveled a lot and had plenty of diversions. For her everything held a memory, an emotional charge for either her daughter or him. It was so hard losing him at a time when she needed his support more than ever.

The Woman was devastated. She could not let go of this man who had awakened so much inside of her, and yet she was consumed by guilt for loving him and for being away when the accident happened. Dark days lay ahead.

Releasing the Illusion of Omnipotence

Amethyst sat back in her chair and starred out the window. Reliving those dark days of so many years ago was still hard, and yet she remembered it like it was yesterday. Finally, that painful episode was all out on paper, and she realized she had just reached a new level of acceptance and letting go by doing that, as well as seeing the events of that time in a somewhat different light.

She thought back on the devastation she felt over losing Lord Sumina at such a difficult time, and how angry she had been at him. She realized now that she had projected a great deal of the pain of the situation onto his leaving in some bizarre way. If only he had stayed in her life, he would have given her support. Would he have? Really? She was now realizing that it would have only been a temporary diversion from the real loss, and a way for her to remain in denial of her daughter's death for a while longer. It would have only prolonged the grief process. As it was, she had been plunged headlong into it.

"God what an abyss of despair I was in at that time," she muttered to herself and shuddered with the emotion that surged through her.

Amethyst woke one morning, several days after writing about Cherie's death feeling that same deep down feeling of agony and dread that she had felt just before she learned of the accident. She took a long walk along the beach and sobbed, as she sent up prayers for the safety of her children and grandchildren one by one. She couldn't find a present reason for the awful feeling. She seemed removed from the feeling, as though witnessing it and yet engulfed by it at the same time. It was not until the next day, when nothing dreadful had happened, and she had discussed the whole episode with Hugh, that she realized what had transpired.

Amethyst had been reading SECRET PATHS[1] a book by Terri Apter which talked about a study of the ways women go through midlife. Her research had shown that because mothers expect themselves to be omnipotent, they take on all the guilt when something happens to one of their children.

"Omnipotence is the fantasy that one can do everything without compromising anything; power is the ability to act effectively in the world as we know it" the book had said. Amethyst pondered the statement for a long time. She realized the reason that statement had effected her so profoundly was because she was still laboring under some of the guilt of the expectation of omnipotence, and it had triggered a residue buried so deeply within her that it had not been released yet.

"Funny" she thought to herself. "Here I thought I had dealt completely with the grief and shame I felt." Now she could see how the combination of reliving that painful, life altering episode again from a totally different vantage point, she had dug into an even deeper layer of herself than she had ever dug before. Now after years of letting go, another remnant of the grief and guilt had surfaced to be released. Interesting how the processes of life continue to go on, she thought to herself, in a never ending spiral of realizations.

"It was so much work, coming to grips with that time in my life," Amethyst said to Hugh. "It is just as much work writing about it. I honestly don't know if I can do it."

Hugh replied "Think about the new revelation you just experienced. You wouldn't have arrived at that if you hadn't written it out. Look at all the lose ends you have been able to pull together. Don't quit now, you are obviously working an important process with your writing."

"Your right, of course," she said, smiling wanly at him. "And you are so encouraging too. What would I do without you!" She hugged him warmly and turned to her writing once more. "Power is the ability to act effectively in the world as we know it" Amethyst repeated to herself. "How did I gain that power? I guess that is the answer I am seeking in this process of writing" she thought to herself.

August Has Lasted Too Long

August has lasted too long

The fires of hell
Burn in the August of my life
With a scorching heat
That sears my heart & mind
As I face the Winds of Frustration
Blowing Sands of Despair
Into my eyes
Blinding me to any beauty that might exist!

I cross the Plains of Reason
A hot, relentless logical desert
Burning my emotions
Leaving me parched, weak
My tears spent
Unable to respond.

Will I exist to see September
To once again be renewed by fresh, brisk air
That enlivens me?
I'm strangling in this Abyss
Choked by the suffocating air of guilt and pain
Leadened emotions
Tortured in a seething cauldron of anguish

How does this oppressive darkness
Transmute into the gold & silver
That transforms the hot August landscape
Into the brilliance of autumn?

Why did you die in the August of my life mon Cherie?
My precious flower
Did the heat of my August wilt you
The very essence of springtime
fresh, innocent, new.

Cut down one miserable August day
Your passing prolonging the torture
And the uncertainty of my August indefinitely.

Did my August frighten you
Was it too intense for your gentle soul?
Or was your leaving
Some preordained supreme test?
And will I make it through this one?

Are you watching me somewhere?
Is that fresh, almost imperceptible
Breeze of hope I feel occasionally
Your way of comforting me?

Was it foreordained
That I must cross these Plains without you?
That we must be tested in this way?
Or a mere accident of fate
That has left us all stunned?

August has lasted too long.

CHAPTER FIVE

THE ABYSS

To the world, The Woman appeared to be handling her grief very well. Inside, she was crumbling. Wretchedness seeped deeper and deeper into her being as the stark realization of the death of one of her beloved children permeated the aftermath of daily life in her family.

She was acutely aware of the children's suffering over the loss of their beloved sister, and she felt helpless to comfort them in any way that was effective.

She struggled with the guilt she felt over loving Ben and her affair with Lord Sumina, and wondered if she was being punished. So many losses to grieve. Her precious child was gone, her marriage was an emotional standoff. She had loved and lost three men.

Her body was tormented by piercing chills of gnawing pervasive self-loathing from her throat to her belly; a constant reminder from the time she awoke in the morning until she slipped into the welcome forgetting of sleep of the emotional nightmare now reigning over her existence.

A numb resoluteness was all that kept her going. She worked, comforted the children the best she could, grieved with her husband, tended the grave, and yearned for Lord Sumina, all the while groping in the dark void that was her existence.

Isolation

Crying, this morning
I face another day
In the clutches of pain
That simply won't go away
I turn to tools that have helped before
in a futile attempt
to break down the door

and escape this prison of malaise

I asked the I Ching for a reason
"Impasse, stagnation, decay"
was all it would say
I skipped workout class
I couldn't bring myself to senseless movement
Then tried Tai Chi
Useless effort to raise my energy
Still the uncompromising isolation
Of brutal senseless separation
incapacitates me

I cry for my child
And the void she's left that nothing can fill
And we didn't get to talk
and now never will.

I wrestle with guilt
Over my feelings of loss
For the lover I yearn for
Unsolicited circumstances
That now forever keep us apart.

I share anguish with my husband
Over our lost child
And the other death
The promise of "happily ever after"
We both know is forever gone.

I am acutely aware of all the events
That have changed my world so much
It will never be the same
I am overcome by grief and shame!

My gut churns with anger
At my child for leaving and putting us through this
(I have my philosophical and accepting moments
but not today)

At a man that I loved
For withdrawing
Leaving me empty, hurt, and lost
At a time when I needed him the most

At my husband
For the hold he has on me
For having so much pain I can't cause anymore
For the guilt he can make me feel
by the things he says.

At myself
For the child I could not protect
For allowing myself to be this vulnerable
At a husband and the power he has over me
At a lost lover that I cannot forget

I lament
A battered body that could not support life
A lover's struggle to protect himself from his own guilt
A father's grief

And I weep
For my own pain and needs and their validity
I wonder about my right to fulfil them
Feeling I must acquiesce to others
At the expense of myself
The price I pay for my transgressions

Today
And for many tomorrows
I'll do the work expected of me
I'll nurture people who need it
I'll go through the motions of life
Suspended in this limbo of grief
Because...
I honestly don't know what else to do.

Consumed with feelings of loneliness, guilt and rejection, The Woman wandered in the Desert of Sadness. A lost soul, alone with seemingly no way out, she found a cave and went inside to rest from the heat of the scorching Fires of Hell that tormented her. The cave was dark, and not seeing a large hole, she fell into it. Sucked through a vortex of darkness she tumbled into a deep abyss. Certainly now she would perish, and she didn't care. She hoped it would be soon, for then she would be released from the unbearable torment she could not escape.

For many days she wandered in the Abyss, weeping inconsolably, terrified of the incredible darkness that had settled over her entire psyche. She was not able to comprehend how people she loved, and circumstances she had trusted could betray her so completely. In this state, she found herself by the dark and murky waters of the Sea of Desperation.

Living in The Sea of Desperation was a dreadful two-headed monster, the Monster of Frustration. One of his heads, Guilty Sorrow formed from the suppressed love The Woman was unable to give to Lord Sumina, or Ben, her anguish from losing them and her guilt for loving someone besides her husband.

In her darkness a small glimmer of realization surfaced when she recognized that all the love she had poured out to Lord Sumina was the suppressed love she had for Ben. Now that avenue of love's expression was also closed to her, and the vengeance of her inexpressible feelings turned on her, becoming a destructive force within her.

The Head of Hopeless Loss grew out of her anguish over her daughter's death and the desolation she felt. She had failed as a parent and hadn't been able to protect her child from death. As the carrier of her pain, this monster writhed in agony, bent on destroying the woman who created him.

As The Woman agonized over the loss of her daughter and lost loves, he grew larger. The monster became tangled in the Seaweed of Oppression when she wondered why the universe would punish her for trying to follow her heart. It was that old whip of wondering if her needs and desires counted at all, and it tore holes in the monster's hide.

Then the Prince, tiring of "charming" princesses, took a long look at the woman he had married and realized how much she meant to him. Especially after the loss of their daughter he admired the strength he saw in her. He told her that she was more beautiful than he could ever remember and that there was not another woman in the world that he would rather be with.

The Monster of Frustration tore at the chains that held him in bondage, for although The Woman cared for the Prince, she no longer loved him.

The Wife Or Expectations

On a bed of obedience
And legal compliance
I served you as wife
And bore your children
And kept your house.

Awed by your arrogance
In my youthful innocence
I saw it as strength
And interpreted your lust
as emotion.
And in my naive yearning for romance
I gave myself to you.

You seduced me
You provided for me
You gave me children
But you did not know how to love me.

In my desperate need to be affirmed
I tried to win your love

57

To make my lonely bed of tears
More joyful.
But you were drunk with the wine
Of the power you had over me
And jeered and ridiculed my pleadings
Making me feel weak
For needing your love.

Immersed in self-loathing
For my weaknesses
I bore my fate
In quiet frustration
For many years
Tending your needs
And the needs of our children.

Until
Miracle of Miracles
one day you said you realized
how much you loved me
And waited expectantly
For my grateful response

But
I surprised us both
By not being able to respond
For I had spent painful years
Letting go
Struggling
Not to love you so
Something in me died
And now it didn't matter anymore.

The only difference is
I won't "jeer" at your "weakness"
For I've suffered the pain
Of loving in vain
And know how it feels.

It's sad
The irony of our timing.

****

The process of writing "The Wife or Expectations" put The Woman's feelings toward the Prince into perspective as she took a long look at how the circumstances in her marriage had developed.

She reminded herself that since he was the father of her children, and she couldn't be with the man she loved she was meant to stay with the Prince. The Head of Frustration grew larger and uglier because she could not show The Prince the love he expected and finally wanted from her.

These monsters bickered and bellered so much, tearing at The Woman's insides so brutally that she began to feel ill. The illness took on the vehemence of a tempestuous storm within her.

The Tempest

The Woman found herself in the middle of a hurricane
Trapped in the center of the storm raging within her
She cried to the Spirit of the Tempest
With tears streaming down her face -

"I live with a man I cannot love
And loved two men I cannot have
I've born 6 children
And stood helplessly by
And watched one die.

"I've learned so many things
My library bulges with books
Silent symbols of my relentless seeking & searching
Others' thoughts I've sought to make my own
Yet answers allude me
And I feel as tho I know nothing.

"I'm aware of people who love me
But it doesn't fill the void and I wonder
What is this relentless yearning that drives me
Creating a gulf between us
And is it worth the struggle?

"In shattered disbelief
I've raged with bitter hurt and angry jealousy
At my husband's lovers
And yearned for my own
Setting myself up to be hurt again & again.

"I have so much pain
I wish I could cut it out of my body
And I don't know what to do!!
I work to help people with their pain
Yet I can't relieve my own.

"I wrestle with the unconscious forces within me
Hoping to understand myself better
My head swims with rationalities
My gut churns with emotion
My psyche feels battered and bruised
And I am tossed in a tempest of confusion."

"I don't want to hurt anymore!" are my anguished cries!
I pound the wall with my fists sobbing "How do I stop this
pain?"
I beg for answers "What have I done to deserve to suffer
like this?"
"I shake with the intensity of the storm within me
Wishing it were powerful enough to annihilate me!"

And the Spirit of the Tempest listened
As the woman raged on and on
Venting the bottled up anger and despair.
It watched,
As each new surge of raw angry emotion
Welled up and filled her being
Dashing against her
As the ocean dashes against the rocks in a storm
Beating against her until she could resist no more.

And the Spirit of the Tempest stood by and did nothing
For it was not time for her to be comforted.

Finally, the storm subsided
The Woman exhausted, slept.

She awoke to find herself still alive
Surprised to feel a sense of strength she had never felt
before.
Tho battered and beaten
She made it to the Eye of the Hurricane
Had begged Death to carry her away
And it had not

So the Woman
With an air of determined resignation
Took a deep breath
And with all the courage she could muster
Opened the door
And stepped out into the Tempest once more.

During that exhausted sleep after the storm, Cherie came to The Woman in a dream. In that dream they talked of the accident and of her death. Cherie reassured her that she was ok and in a good place. The Woman awoke from the dream with the gentle powerful memory of the dream and her beautiful daughter, and for the first time since the accident, she felt some comfort.

As The Woman began to pull herself together after the storm, the Old One appeared at her side. After a joyful cry of recognition mixed with relief and a long comforting hug from the Old One, they walked and talked, and he brought her to the edge of The Abyss.

"I have been watching over you," he said. "One of the most important aspects of the Journey on the Plains of Reason is the experiences you have through the choices you make and the development you achieve from them. I could not intervene to stop the events that transpired, but I can help you to escape the hold those Monsters of Frustration have on you. I have come to guide you if you will allow me. Your experiences hold such a store of richness to be gleaned. Will you let me help you?"

"Oh please," said The Woman. "I've felt so ashamed of what I have done I wondered if you would ever have anything to do with me again. I have felt too much shame to go to the Tower and ask for help. I am so relieved to see you!"

"One must at times go to the darkest of places for the light of a destined path to be seen." he said gently.

"Until now The Tower has served as a place of solace and refuge for you to hide and do inner work. In The Tower you found a place to retreat apart from your everyday life.

"The Tower also serves another purpose, however. Once one finds The Tower and begins to retreat there, a reordering of your world begins. Your old way of life and thinking must come to an end for a new order to insert itself. At the same time, you are required to follow through to the consequences of your choices. Mixed in with your choices is the process begun by your visits to The Tower.

"This journey has great power and takes on a life of its' own at a certain point. You have arrived at the inevitable stage of the DEATH Archetype. The force of this Archetype passes through everyone's life many times and in many forms as one's life progresses through levels of learning. Each new level of attainment is reached when you work through and let go of the the former level. Life and death are partners in this World of Polarity. Out of death comes life and out of life comes death.

"Here is a mystery. One day you can transcend both. That ability lies in a potential future, if you continue your ascension up the spiral of this path. Keep the promise of going beyond life and death close to your heart, and continue with the work that needs to be done now.

"Always keep in mind that things are not as they seem. Much of your pain was caused by being caught in the bondage of expectations, yours and of those around you and your need to maintain outer appearances.

"Why do you feel you have to hide your grief from the world? What beliefs do you have that keep your feelings so locked up?

"I don't like to inflict my problems on other people, and I have a difficult time trusting people with my innermost thoughts and feelings," she replied.

"How do you feel when someone trusts you with a personal problem or sorrow, and you are able to listen or suggest something that really helps them?" he asked.

"I feel good about helping people, and I usually learn something about myself in the process" she answered.

"Don't you think people who love you deserve the same opportunity of learning something about themselves and feeling good by helping you with your problems or just listening?" he responded.

"Well, yes I guess so" she said hesitantly, a light slowly dawning on her. "It is just that I was taught to be independent and self-sufficient."

"Self-sufficiency can be a virtue, it also can be self-righteous pride" he admonished. "Think about that for awhile. You need to ask yourself some questions about what Ben and Lord Sumina represented to you," he went on. "What mirror did they hold? These are issues you will need to work on in The Tower. As you come to understand the mirror these men held up to you, you will vanquish the two-headed monster that has you captive right now.

"In the months to come those questions and your daughter's passing will be the subjects we will continue to explore when you are ready to work again. It would be good for you to pull the DEATH[1] card the next time you visit The Tower. Until then, remember you are loved and guided, and your beliefs create your perception of your world." With those words he faded and was gone.

Dissolution

"Dissolution works on the heart ...to release buried emotions that conceal or distort our true nature. Basically, this means showing our pain and revealing our wounds...It is an unconscious process in which our conscious mind allows the surfacing of previously buried material."

The Emerald Tablet
Dennis William Hauck

Lark Aleta Ferguson

CHAPTER SIX

PEARL DIVING[1] IN THE SEA OF DESPERATION

SHOULD IS A CHAIN OF BONDAGE
OUGHT AN ILLUSION OF THOUGHT
FEAR THE UGLY OPPRESSOR
HAVING POWER OVER THE CHAINS

AWARENESS OF UNCONSCIOUS SHOULDS
BREAKS THE OUGHTS OF GENERATIONS
FREEING US FROM THE CHAINS
OF DISTORTED PERCEPTIONS.

It took The Woman almost a year after Cherie's death to arrive at the place in the Abyss where the Old One came to her and told her to work with the DEATH card.

She pulled the card as instructed and remembered the teaching of The Old One, that the "death" the card symbolized is a transformational process, in which a new order is inserting itself. She struggled with that concept. It was a terrible sacrifice to lose a child to death as part of a new order. Couldn't it have been accomplished some other way? She labored under a heavy weight of guilt for her part in this. If she had never found the Tower, would this have happened? These thoughts plagued her through sleepless nights and endless days. Was this "new order" really worth it?

Her entire family suffered. Each one in their own way tried to make some sense of the emotional ordeal they were forced to endure, none of them possessing the skills to verbalize their feelings or knowing how to deal with them, each confronted with the endless finality of the loss of their beloved Cherie and the hole it rent in the family.

The younger children were not able to concentrate, and their school work suffered, a reflection of the anguish and inexpressible grief living inside each child. Sunny, the sister next to Cherie in age, began to get into trouble as she acted out the anger she felt at losing her older sister. The Woman felt helpless in the shadow of the dark cloud that hung over her family, casting a gray hue on the events of their everyday world.

It was this state of affairs, shortly after she pulled the DEATH CARD, when The Woman learned of a two week retreat in a town several hours travel away. It was based on a process called Psychosynthesis.[2] She wasn't sure what it meant, but it sounded interesting, and she hoped the information would hold some help or comfort. She was feeling a strong need to get away in hopes of seeing the situation a little differently. She made the the arrangements to attend.

It was hard for her to leave her children again, especially after what had happened the last time she left them, but she felt so lifeless inside, she knew she must get help. She discussed going with the Old One. He strongly encouraged her to go, reminding her that the only person she could heal or change was herself, and she would be of more help to her family by seeking her own healing than by staying there in the pool of suffering. Something had to turn them in a different direction.

Diving

Manna House[3] was a retreat center for all faiths, maintained by Catholic Nuns. It had a large meeting and dining room on the main floor and an upstairs dormitory where the participants stayed.

The Woman settled into the small but comfortable room that was to be her home for the next two weeks and prepared to meet for the evening meal and get acquainted session which was the activity scheduled for that first evening. She met the nineteen other participants and 4 facilitators that were to be her fellow sojourners on the journey ahead.

During the two weeks that followed, The Woman was introduced to several schools of psychological thought. It was there that she began the process of bringing those teachings into a core of eclectic knowledge that would continue to assist her in her journey of self discovery for the rest of her life. It also was there that she was introduced to the concept of "Shadow" which would soon open deep inner doors for her.

The morning sessions consisted of a discussion on the subject for the day, a group guided imagery and small group discussion of individual experiences in the imagery. In the afternoons individual sessions were scheduled so that each participant had the opportunity to experience private more in-depth guided imagery with one of the facilitators.

"The Kingdom of God is a commitment to an inner way. It is full of self-confrontation and helps you prioritize inner values with outer values. Your seeking of this Kingdom will bring to you your own wholeness and give your life endeavors spiritual meaning so the rewards of the Kingdom can be felt in this life" the instructor began.

"Those who are called upon to enter the kingdom may not always recognize what is happening to them. At first it may seem dark and dreadful, because the first experiences are a darkening of our old state of mind in order for a new consciousness to emerge. If the Kingdom is to emerge in your being, this old person must die, and the walls built by the ego which hide the Inner Self must be torn down. When these defenses are battered down forcibly by the movement within, it may at first seem like a violent assault. The nature of the Kingdom is very demanding, and our entrance into it frequently involves crisis. All of the old person and old attitudes are challenged by the Kingdom."

Dying of an old self. My life had been so predictable until the events that started with Ben changed everything so drastically I didn't know who I was anymore, or where I belonged.

The Woman was brought out of her reverie by the words of the instructor.

"Most therapeutic approaches rely on words to release you from your emotional prisons. The use of imagery the language of the unconscious and of feeling is often more efficient as a way to open locked doors to forgotten feelings and experiences. Images are the language of the imagination, pictures, sounds, feelings, tastes, and smells that you can construct rather than experience directly through the senses.

"Traveling in the realm of imagination is intrinsically healing for several reasons. It demands a certain level of relaxation. Exploring your own flow of images allows you to glimpse what issues are pressing for further attention. Working through your emotional blocks on an imaginal level can relieve symptoms and produce personality and attitude changes. Your imagination is psychological space where you can monitor the stirrings of your subconscious mind as well as rehearse behavior. If you can imagine something, you can do it.

"Deeply felt imaginal experiences can change your feeling and sense of self. When you imagine something vividly, using as many of your imaginal senses as you can muster, you are creating a real psychological event. If you do it vividly, using your full bodied imagination, you will be setting off the same reactions in your psyche and nervous system that you would in a real situation. Such an experience can serve several healing functions.

"Often times, working on an imagery level before an encounter with someone with whom you have unfinished business releases much of the negative energy, and the encounter can be more positive. On a more subtle level, such as an issue involving a person that is no longer in your life, or living, an encounter in imagery can convince your subconscious mind that a real confrontation has taken place. and a shift in your perspective can result."

"THE MIND'S EYE ACCEPTS AS TRUTH WHAT IT SEES IN IMAGERY, AS WELL AS WHAT IT SEES IN THE PHYSICAL WORLD. WORK DONE IN MEDITATION IS AS REAL AS A LIFE EXPERIENCE BECAUSE THAT'S WHERE THE FEELINGS ARE!!"

For their first exercise, the group was guided to find themselves in a home and locate where they were in that home and what they were feeling.

"I am in the cellar of my childhood home. I am terrified and frustrated standing at the bottom of the stairs screaming"... The Woman wrote in her journal following the imagery. "The stairs...are the way out of the Abyss, this cellar. My feelings are important. I feel, I feel, I feel, I feel empty. I'm paralyzed, I can't move myself. I have no place to go. I feel empty or full of something I can't cough up that is blocking my feelings. I feel so fragmented."

After the imagery during the group processing time, each participant shared what they felt comfortable with about their experience in the imagery. Their facilitator's name was Joselyn.

The Woman talked about being in the basement of her childhood home, which really wasn't a basement but a dark and dank cellar. The group discussion pointed to several potential directions she might explore in the following days, regarding those images. Joselyn explained that the childhood home pointed in the direction of starting from "home base" so to speak. The cellar eluded to what was hidden, i.e. unconscious issues that began in childhood.

She was very reluctant to continue when during the first individual session, the repressed memory of a step-father who had molested her surfaced. Her mother was only married to him for a short time, and he died while she was still a child. She had hidden that series of episodes deep within her and had made a promise to herself never to talk about it. Now in this safe and accepting environment, it surfaced. Joselyn explained to her that it was time for her to begin looking at it and encouraged her to continue. Together they gave the small child within her who had endured the violation ways of safely confronting the man and the situation. The Woman was surprised at the intensity of this imagery session and the powerful feelings it generated. Afterward, Joselyn explained to her that she would experience subsequent realizations and have to work more deeply on this issue as time went on, but she felt The

Woman had made considerable progress in bringing the repressed emotions and shame out of their hiding place. The acknowledgement of this issue was a huge first step.

Over the course of her stay at Manna House, The Woman had several experiences Joselyn explained to her were "leadings" or events perceived is such a way as to take her in a new direction.

The Woman's grandfather has been raised Catholic, but when he married her grandmother, he left the church because she refused to join or raise her children as Catholics. Her grandmother held a great deal of prejudice toward the Catholic Church, and her studies and findings had deepened that prejudice over the years. As The Woman mused about this, she realized that even though her grandfather never spoke of it, grandmother's hatred of his spiritual heritage must have been a source of pain for him. She was feeling that in some way her experiences here were reconciling this schism in the collective consciousness of her family. She didn't know what the dynamics were, but she knew that deep inside some kind of familial healing was taking place. She prayed for this realization to be so.

***

The Woman lay on her bed one evening, ruminating over all that had played a part in the pervasive numbness holding her captive. Her thoughts drifted off into the memory of her early experiences with religion.

"How strange" she thought to herself, "that I find myself in a Catholic sponsored gathering which is having such a powerful impact on me. Grandma would turn over in her grave if she knew!"

When The Woman was in her early twenties, years before she discovered The Tower, she became involved with a church that taught that since Jesus kept the Jewish Holy Days, then if we were to be "true" followers of Him, we should also keep those Holy Days, along with accepting Jesus as our personal saviour. It taught that the Christian Holidays were of Pagan origin, forced on civilization in the third century AD by the Catholic Church and that they were wrong to observe. Her grandmother had also uncovered

71

similar information, so of course, initially, The Woman felt that she had found the "True" church.

The church taught exclusivity, which troubled her greatly. She knew so many people outside the church, who were kind and lovingand very spiritual, and yet this church taught that they were lost if they did not believe as the church taught.

Later events that happened internally within the church disillusioned her further on the whole idea of organized churchianity being God ordained. As she became more in touch with how oppressed she was within the structure of that church, she realized that if this was what the "Kingdom of God" was about, she would rather be annihilated than be a part of it. It was a dreadfully confusing time for her, because this church taught that any questioning was a "bad attitude," and intuition was not to be trusted. Only an ordained minister would have the "right" answers.

She struggled for many months, vacillating between self-berating for her bad attitude and a deep gnawing within her telling her that something was very wrong with what was being taught. With the help of one of the ministers, under the auspices of a "study group" who was asking himself the same questions, she and the Prince began to slowly break free of the hold the church had on them. Eventually, they along with about a third of the membership left the church at one time. This movement happened nationwide through out the church.

The church taught that the ones who left were the prophesied "great falling away" that was to happen just before the second coming of Christ. The church had instructed remaining members to shun the ones who left as the "fallen ones." The most painful part was losing the many friends she had made while a member of that church.

Even though the whole episode turned The Woman away from organized religion, it did not turn her away from seeking a spiritual path that made sense to her. Instead, it intensified in her a desire to search for truth. It was then that she had made a decision that God would have to understand when she didn't, forgive her if she took some wrong turns and lead her to understanding. She asked to be guided, and when an idea or concept attracted her, she accepted it as the direction she was to go. There were answers "out there" somewhere that would feed her cravings for a spiritual life, and she would find them. She called herself a"Spiritual Vagabond" and would not join or affiliate herself with any religious organization.

She was realizing as she mused that she had left churchianity behind, but a great deal of the internal controls she had been trained in remained imbedded into her belief system and her approach to the world. She drifted off to sleep thinking to herself she must explore that realization more in the near future, and she wondered if that wasn't part of what the Old One was talking to her about in the Abyss...

The Woman was intrigued by all the childhood and early adulthood issues that surfaced during her stay, but she was feeling a strong sense of urgency to work on the pressing issues that had brought her to Manna House. She had arrived in such turmoil about her current life and was desperate to find some answers to her present dilemmas. She expressed this to Joselyn, who explained to her that the present would not heal until the pain was released from the past, and the past would only leave when the gifts were gleaned from the experiences. Joselyn encouraged her by explaining to her that she was doing an immense amount of work, even though it didn't seem like it at the time. She also reassured her that the process would address all that was in her psyches' agenda before she left. "Give yourself time," Joselyn encouraged. "We aren't finished yet," and smiled, knowingly. She had seen the process work many times and knew there was more in store for The Woman.

A Gift of Compassion

It was a huge leap for The Woman to find herself in a Christian/ Catholic setting. It was even a bigger stretch for her to allow Jesus into her inner world, but into it He came.

73

It was afternoon, time for her final private session with Joselyn. She settled in on a couch in the room, closed her eyes and began to relax, listening to Joselyn's soothing voice as she guided The Woman to her safe place.

The Woman found herself sitting on a bench in a small garden sanctuary similar to the Missions she had visited in Southern California when she was a child. The surroundings felt ancient and held a deep sense of serenity and peace that put her at ease instantly.

She looked up to see The Old One standing in front of her. He greeted her and told her that he had brought someone to her who wanted to spend some time with her. As he said that, an Image that looked like a composite of all the pictures she had ever seen of Jesus appeared in front of her. As He appeared, the image of the Old One smiled at her, faded and disappeared.

Light radiated from this Being's Countenance, and The Woman felt at peace instantly with Him. He held out his hand, she took it and stood up. They began walking in the garden. As they walked, The Woman found herself tearfully venting all the pentup feelings she had been carrying inside of her for such a long time.

She talked about how unfair it was to raise a child and see her blossom into a beautiful young woman, and before they had the opportunity to experience all that wonder she had become, she was violently stopped. She sobbed as she expressed her feelings of guilt at being away when the accident happened.

She expressed her anguish at the possibility that her daughter's death was some kind of punishment to get her to her knees and how she couldn't bear being responsible for her daughter's death for the rest of her life and how strongly she felt she was responsible.

The Being held her as sobs from deep inside wrenched through her body. She sobbed in His arms for a very long time.

Finally, she was able to become quiet, and the Being spoke. He spoke to her about many things. He talked about the powerful forces at work when one is on a path searching for truth. He explained that as she experienced separation from her Source Self into earth life, she gradually became ensnared into belief systems that held her trapped in a limiting mindset. It was inevitable that she would be brought to some kind of crisis powerful enough to rock the foundation of those belief systems in order to make her question her belief structure and look outside of it for answers. This would give Source a way to reach her and help her expand her awareness. If she allowed the changes to take hold in her, Source would eventually work through her on the earth plane.

He explained to her that each person has their own plan when they arrive on this earth, even one's children.

"Cherie's death accelerated the individual journeys of those who were close to her and intensified the process of whatever that individual came to learn," He went on to explain. "For some the exploration would take them deeper into spiritual seeking and awareness. For others it might prove to them that there is no higher help, and the rest of their lives will be spent in bitterness fully experiencing separation, a decision they had made to explore in depth long before they were born."

"Cherie is not just your child. She is a spiritual being just as you are, with her own purposes and explorations on the earth and beyond the earth planes to fulfill. Her decision to leave early was her ultimate gift to you. Your gift to her is what you do with her gift. People leave the earth plane through the process you call death every day. In their passing they leave something for those left behind to wrestle and grow from. Your daughter's life did not end with her leaving," He assured her.

"Keep in mind, there are no guarantees when someone comes to be with you how long they will stay," He reminded her. "A basic destiny blueprint and free choice are powerful polarities at work on this planet, and they interact to manifest events into your lives" He explained to her.

The Woman wept with intense feelings of relief, for the Being emanated a powerful resonance of deep comfort as He spoke to her. He helped her understand how much of what she struggled with were irrational belief systems, based on teachings created to cause guilt and fear, not truth. His last words to her were "keep in mind that things are not always as they seem," and as he said those words, His image began to fade, and she was once again sitting with The Old One on a bench in the garden of the sanctuary.

Back in her room, The Woman wrote of the afternoon's events. As she sat at her desk writing in her journal, she felt more peace than she had felt since Cherie's passing.

She was in awe of all the Being had said to her. She wrote for hours trying to remember every word and detail. The teaching she had received helped to give her an entirely different way of integrating her daughter's death. As she wrote and pondered the day's events, some other realizations began to surface.

"The feeling of having the Christ Being come right away, the image was very detailed and very powerful, and the garden was such a comforting and peaceful place. Now I am seeing that seeking the Kingdom within really is a process of taking Christ's teachings and applying them to realizations from the inner world. I wonder if Christ's 'second coming' will ever be a literal physical event. I am beginning to think that it is a state of mind, this second coming. A "Christ consciousness", an understanding and internal awareness that takes place in people's lives in the process of self transformation. If that is so, then it is possible that the 'end of the world' happens again and again individually as people restructure their personalities, allowing obsolete parts of themselves to die, and new parts of themselves to be born. This way they are building their 'treasures in heaven.' The gifts of the kingdom becomes a process of cultivating inner values and treasures of the spirit, creating inner wealth."

As she sat at her desk writing in her journal, a pair of doves landed on the window sill in her room. She watched them for a long time, transfixed by their presence, weeping as the emotion of the experience spilled out in tears of release. They symbolized affirmation of the work she was doing and she felt a deep gratitude for their gentle presence.

Resurfacing

The Woman left Manna House reluctantly and tearfully. She had sojourned with 23 other people, all seeking a way to heal and find their way into the kingdom. She had experienced a deep and genuine meeting of minds, and it felt like a coming home to her. There in a safe and loving cocoon she took some giant steps on the long road Home in the healing work she had started.

In the course of the two weeks she had become aware of repressed feelings of betrayal she had experienced through organized religion and the beliefs instilled in her that determined many of her reactions to life events.

The Woman now more than ever, was determined to continue her search and study of other spiritual belief systems, but she was more at peace with organized churchianity. She was beginning to accept the concept that all paths would eventually lead to God. It was apparent to her that the seeking was the most important part. Seeking and intent. "God looked at the heart," she remembered from her bible days, and that thought continued to comfort her.

"Seek first the kingdom of God, and all these things will be added." Those words still resonated with her and now took on a much deeper meaning to her. She would continue to seek as long as she lived, of that she was sure.

The Woman realized that her years of intense bible study while in the church had given her a solid foundation from which to reach out and now understood the reason for her time spent with that belief system, enabling her to move into a place of gratitude. Those experiences had prepared her to receive this precious gift of help. She also realized she was learning valuable lessons in discernment. Glean the love from the teachings and let the rest go as "doctrines of men." She remembered an admonition she had heard in her church days about "teaching for commandments the doctrines of men." That exhortation now carried a deeper meaning. Her task ahead would be one of sorting out many more doctrines in search of truth.

She was helped to put her daughter's death within a framework that she could live with. She wasn't through grieving by any means; but she had been deeply comforted and carried new strength in her heart.

She had started to work on letting go of Lord Sumina. That would still take some time, but some ground work had been laid, and she now had some tools to work with to go deeper into understanding the dynamics of that relationship.

The road ahead was still long, but she now had tools to help her understand and the hope that she would eventually completely heal from the accumulated pain that had held her in bondage for so much of her life. She also left with a promise of a Kingdom within. She wasn't exactly sure what the promise entailed but somehow knew it was the ideal she would be seeking in her continuing work.

Synchronicities Gift

Amethyst sat watching the surf play on the sand and mused for a long time after writing about her experiences at Manna House. She had just been reading about synchronicities in a book titled *The Cosmic Game* by Stanislav Grof in which he quoted Jung, who defined synchronicity as a "simultaneous occurrence of a psychic state with one or more external events which appear as meaningful parallels to the momentary subjective state."

Now, so many years later she was able to see how magnificently the worlds of objectivity and subjectivity had blended during those weeks at Manna House. An entire new level of significance gave her a thrill of realization as she thought of the leadings and the doves and how her outer world had actually reflected back to her symbols from her inner world. She realized that during her stay those worlds had actually merged, serving to make the events during that time deeply memorable and important. Now, in the writing of the events she was given yet another gift in seeing the powerful illustrations of the workings of synchronicity. "Spiral, endless spiral" she thought to herself.

Amethyst reflected for a long time on the specific incidents that presented themselves in imagery during that magical time. It was as though some inner driving impulse was determined to put her in touch with as many deep seated issues as she could tolerate during that two week window of time. She felt a chill go up her spine as she realized why. She had arrived at Manna House with her defenses weakened, laboring under the heavy burden of guilt and grief. She didn't have the energy to repress those issues, and they were able to surface. Of course, this was a wonderful opportunity for issues that needed to be addressed to leave her unconscious and drift into her field of conscious awareness to be dealt with. "And the theme?" she mused to herself. "Shame, pure and simple." She had been forced to acknowledge a deep and painful overlay of shame which served as a filter through which she experienced every aspect of her sexuality, her gender and her sense of self.

Lark Aleta Ferguson

MAYA'S [4]DREAM

You asked for a chance
at earthly life
"An experience of separation
in order to grow" you said
So
God took a deep breath
blew a poignant sigh
a long lingering good bye
and sent you on your way

A release of soul
A quickening of body
A journey into Maya's dream
To the world of imagining

Fly Fly Dearest One
Into the world of dark and sun
Your endless journey has begun

You may experience sorrow and pain
before you return home again
The world you seek is bittersweet
Some even call it bleak

Your life's task
a plan unique
For you are destined to gently speak
To all who you touch
Of loves' strength and wonder

And when it is your time to leave
Those who have known you will grieve
As they remember
Cherished private moments
of your walk with each

Each dear precious wing

who comes from beyond imagining
into the world of light and dark
leaves a stamp of Essence's Spark
and a corner of the world is changed.

And now we stand at Parting's door
As you again take wing and fly
back to the Heart of Unity once more
To stand on heaven's floor.

So fly, fly Little wing
Your legacy a precious offering
Your mystery a poignant pondering.
For those of us remaining in Maya's Dream.

Separation

"Separation retrieves frozen energy released from the breaking down of habits and crystallized thoughts (assumptions, beliefs, and prejudices) and hardened feelings. (emotional blockages, neuroses, and phobias). This misspent energy is now available to drive our spiritual transformation.

The Emerald Tablet
Dennis William Hauck

CHAPTER SEVEN

LUMINA AND THE TEMPLE OF THE MOON

The Woman returned home from Manna House with a renewed sense of hope and just in time for an overnight camping and canoe trip her husband had planned to take her and the children on. The Woman's brother and his family would also join them. They would rent canoes at their destination and take a picnic lunch to eat in the middle of the day, somewhere along the river.

It was the first real outing the family had planned since Cherie's death, and The Woman found herself looking forward to it with eager anticipation. She had returned determined to somehow help with the healing of her family, and this seemed like a good start. They reached their camp site in the early evening, with plenty of time to pitch their tents and eat a simple evening meal. It was an Indian Summer night. The sky was clear, the stars created a bright canopy of twinkling lights. The air was cool and crisp enough for a campfire which cast its cheerful, dancing warmth on this hopeful gathering. They sat around the campfire, chatting and roasting marshmallows, and for a wonderful precious evening the family felt whole. They were looking forward with great anticipation to the trip in the morning. Finally, the children climbed into their tents and fell asleep. The Prince and The Woman's brother had taken a walk down by the river and were sitting on the bank chatting.

The Woman wandered off on her own and found a bank where she could sit and absorb the splendor of the evening. The light of the full harvest moon danced on the water.

"I name you River of Hope," she said softly to the water as it merrily babbled over the rocks. She found herself musing about how even in the midst of pain there is still such incredible beauty in the world. In fact, she thought, the beauty was even more exquisite because of its ability to exist in spite of the pain.

Her mind wandered off to The Tower and the events she had set in motion by going there. Now she had experienced rich inner events at Manna House. She thought about how The Tower had been a catalyst to her inner world and was still a welcome retreat from the world. At the same time, she was learning to access her inner world anywhere she was. That fact was vividly illustrated to her during her stay at Manna House.

As she sat there absorbed in the moon's spell, almost as if in response to her train of thought, she felt a tingling sensation shimmer through her body. It became so strong that she began to shiver, even though she wasn't cold. It was almost as if she could consciously feel the blood coursing through her veins. A strong mist surrounded her, she felt a whirling sensation and the next thing she knew she was sitting on a stone bench in a garden surrounded by a temple starkly silhouetted against the direct light of the full harvest moon.

The Woman turned toward the sound of footsteps, to see a figure emerging from the temple. As the figure came closer, she beheld a tall, radiant and luminous woman. She and the temple seemed to come out of the Moon itself. The young woman had an aloof air of virginal detachment about her, seemingly uncontaminated by the experience of earthly life. She had long dark hair that shimmered in the moonlight. Her eyes were a deep azure blue and had a very penetrating quality to them. Her skin was the color of delicate porcelain. She was dressed in a long white gown, covered by a long, flowing cape the same color as her eyes.

"Greetings," she said to the The Woman. "I am Lumina, High Priestess of Feminine Essence. I guard the Mysteries of the Feminine Soul. The Old One said that you would be coming. Your arrival tells me you are ready to begin our work together."

The Woman listened to her in speechless awe as Lumina went on to explain

"It will be my job to guide you to understand that which is holy and virginal within yourself and to help you learn to trust again.

"The loss of your daughter burdened you with unnecessary guilt. Her passing from your world served many purposes, some you are now only beginning to understand. I trust you will continue to find comfort from your discoveries.

"Tonight the time has come for us to explore an area which is very important to your overall growth and development. So far your experiences with men have been painful and difficult, have they not?" she asked.

"Yes, and I have grown to dislike and mistrust them" retorted The Woman.

"Your feelings are certainly understandable," replied Lumina "but there is so much that you are not aware of that has contributed to your experience. It will be my task, with your permission and attention to reflect back to you several big pieces of the picture you would benefit from seeing in a slightly different light."

Lumina turned and began to walk down a path in the garden away from The Woman. "Follow me" she said.

The Woman stood up from the stone bench she was sitting on and followed Lumina down a narrow winding path. They had walked quite a distance when the path opened up onto a breathtaking meadow, alive with wild flowers in crimson oranges and brilliant yellows and fuschia pinks. The landscape was filled with vibrant color, gently rolling hills, and ancient gnarled Oak trees dotting the horizon looking like giant bonsai trees.

The Woman drank in the cool brisk air, immersed in the splendor, and for a moment felt an incredible sense of freedom like a tremendous burden had been lifted. Tears filled her eyes, and she trembled with the poignancy of the moment, as she sensed the exhilaration as a hint of a future freedom, not one existing in her present life.

They walked through the meadow for what seemed like hours and a moment at the same time, walking toward a mountain a short distance away. As they came closer, a waterfall came into view, breathtaking as it cascaded over the huge rocks and boulders making its way down the side of the mountain.

Lumina said, "that mountain is a reflection of the journey you are on. The waterfall cuts a new path down the mountain, just as your tears are cutting a new path of realization for you. The water from the pool at the bottom of the falls flows to the River of Hope, where you began the journey of this night."

The Woman followed Lumina as she walked toward the pool. Lumina instructed The Woman to bathe in the pool. Following Lumina's guidance, The Woman removed her garments, laying them on a rock by the pool and gingerly lowered her body into the water. As she sank into the water, she felt an overwhelming surge of gut wrenching sorrow course through her entire body. She let out an agonized cry and started to climb out of the water, but Lumina encouraged her to stay with what she was feeling.

At that moment an image of Lord Sumina appeared, and The Woman's heart began to pound. His demeanor remained very controlled as he struggled to express to The Woman the guilt and conflict he suffered over his relationship with her and asked her to let go of him. The Woman resisted, sobbing.

"Where will I direct all these feelings I have for you, if I cannot give them to you?" she whispered through her tears.

Lord Sumina just looked at her, maintaining his stoic demeanor. He would not give her any encouragement.

Lumina turned to The Woman and spoke to her in a very firm voice, explaining that all the emotional energy that she was spending on Lord Sumina was depleting her life force. She helped her to see how the constant mourning for him had become an emotional addiction, an endless loop of pain which was blocking out much of her ability to pay attention and to grow, causing her to stagnate.

"You live in a world of shadows on the earth plane," Lumina said. "When those shadows are unacknowledged and projected, they become enemies of choice. Understanding what you are doing is the beginning of self knowledge, and to the extent that you can recognize and utilize the projections as mirrors is to the extent that you will experience freedom from those projections and the pain they produce.

"It is time to withdraw your focus on him and utilize it to find the part of yourself that Lord Sumina represents," she went on to explain. "His purpose in your life has been to help you see what is really in you and draw it out."

The Woman was intrigued by what Lumina was explaining to her. "You mean he represents a part of myself?" she gasped. At the moment that she uttered those words, the image of Lord Sumina began to fade.

"Exactly," Lumina replied. "The longing that is in your heart for Lord Sumina is really the longing of that part of you that he represents to be recognized, expressed and integrated into your being. His name is Animus. and he is a part of that unknown or shadow part of yourself."

"The feeling of freedom that you felt in the Meadow is the way you will feel when you have let go of the person, Lord Sumina, and have integrated the spirit of what he represents to you."

With that Lumina scooped some of the mud from the pool where the Life Force of Emotion flowed into the River of Hope and placed it on The Woman's heart as a poultice. The Woman felt the mud draw the ache from her heart allowing her to experience what it felt like to be free from her yearning for Lord Sumina. The image of Lord Sumina disappeared completely, and she felt the projected energy return into her body. A strange feeling of completeness washed over her, and she knew a fragment of her psyche had returned home.

"This is one of many initiations[2] you will experience as you travel the Path of Return," said Lumina.

She went on to explain that Animus is the Male Part of her Psyche. "Animus has many shapes, he can appear as an old man, or as a little boy, as your lover, or a learned teacher, a god or a devil. What you long for in a man, he may appear as.

"He can be both positive and negative and to have a true relationship with him you must discover all that he is in you and integrate him into your conscious understanding.

"Animus can throw light into dark corners of your psyche. He can help you to focus your ideas and give them form. He is a part of your Shadow when he is unrecognized and unexpressed, and he will project his qualities onto a man to get your attention and lure you into his web of seduction.

"Where you got into trouble, and may I add, predictable trouble, was seeing in Lord Sumina many of the talents that you possess and instead of developing them in yourself, you worshiped them in him. Naturally, you would feel that you needed him to live. Do you see how powerful the process of projection can be?" She asked. "You project out of yourself onto someone to whom you are attracted the qualities you want and have within yourself."

The Woman's face wrinkled up in disbelief at that statement, and she started to object. Lumina ignored the interruption and went on.

"You can't recognize qualities you don't have, and you are not attracted to qualities that don't resonate within your own being.

"The projection enables you to experience the qualities you have by seeing them in the other person or reject that which you dislike in yourself by projecting them onto someone you dislike and then feeling repulsion toward that person. The problem is, projection keeps both the best and worst of you outside of yourself and keeps you fragmented. To become 'whole' and at peace with yourself you must recognize the projections for what they are and accept them as a part of yourself. This process is called integration. Your task is to see and integrate both the light and dark within yourself," Lumina explained.

She went on, "Once you have allowed Animus to have an active part in your life you will arrive at a deeper sense of the wholeness in yourself. You will be developing a relationship with the male principle within you. As you do that, you will discover your own creativity and focus. You will no longer live in the shadow of the men you love, or be their shadow. You will be a whole, creative being in your own right."

"Do you see that by becoming Lord Sumina's secret lover, you play the part of his female shadow? You force him to keep the female part of himself unattainable, in the shadows. He cannot fully embrace all within himself which you represent to him as long as you accept his projection of Anima. The circumstances which brought you together were ripe with powerful archetype projections. You were never destined to be mates. You were destined to be catalysts for each other. Do you understand?"

The Woman nodded her head, tentatively. Her head was swimming with the incredible richness of it all. This was a great deal to ponder.

"I have given you much to think about and assimilate. Remember before you met Ben, you pulled THE LOVERS card? Your first encounter with that Energy set you up for this time when you would complete the work on a deeper level with that Essence. Now our work can bring you back to a virginal state. Not the state of youthful innocence, but like a virgin forest, mature, ripe with possibility, your full, true self. With tonight's experiences and your intentions you have made great strides."

The next thing The Woman knew, she was again sitting on the banks by the River of Hope, and for an instant a picture flashed in her mind of THE HIGH PRIESTESS[1] card and quickly faded. She made a mental note to herself to pull the card when she had time in the Tower.

The Woman felt a wave of sadness because she knew that she would never see Lord Sumina again. It was a peaceful sadness, however, because she had a task before her to find Animus and befriend him, and she had the memory of that incredible feeling of freedom that was promised to her. That was indeed something to work for.

She reluctantly got up from her perch on the river bank and walked back to the campsite. The Prince was sitting on a log by the fire and looked up and smiled at her as she walked over to the campfire and sat beside him. She smiled back at him and put her head on his shoulder, as a feeling of bittersweet poignancy shivered through her body.

For the congress of men
For the procreation of children
Makes virgins women

But when God begins to associate with the soul
He brings to pass that she who was formerly woman
Becomes Virgin again

Philo of Alexandria

CHAPTER EIGHT

EMBRACING ANIMUS

The Woman sat in her room in the Tower, holding the picture of THE HIGH PRIESTESS, meditating about all that had transpired with Lumina in the Temple of the Moon.

Lumina had instructed her to continue writing to help integrate the information she had received about Animus. She promised to guide and inspire The Woman in those explorations in order for her to continue to understand on deeper levels the part that Animus and projection played in her life.

The Woman also did as Lumina suggested and pulled THE LOVERS card. She was in territory now where she needed the guidance of both Archetypes.

Once again invoked, the Essence of the LOVERS card would affect her for many months to come as she sorted out the relationships she had experienced and their impact on her. Lumina remained closely accessible to help her, for the time had come for her to make some critical choices between the roads she would take. Would she continue with the husband of her youth and the material comforts he provided her, or would she seek "The Kingdom" first and trust the promise that "all things would be added" if she was faithful to that seeking.

She still had children at home, and the thought of trying to support them and raise them on her own was indeed a sobering thought. She continued to try and rekindle the love she once had for The Prince, but it just was no longer there, and to go on in a marriage that left her emotionally and spiritually cold and live in a relationship where trust no longer existed was against everything she believed life was about.

It was during this period of intense sorting that The Woman had a powerful experience that helped her immensely in her decision making process. It was shortly after her first experience with Lumina and happened one night while she was working with THE HIGH PRIESTESS card. She had lived through a very difficult week and was feeling very depressed and stuck. She had been crying in frustration, struggling with how she could go on with her life.

She closed her eyes, took a few deep breathes, and soon she began to drift. It was a pleasant feeling, this drifting.

The Bridge

The Woman found herself walking down a deserted road. Off to the side, her eyes caught a glimpse of a well. She was very thirsty, so she walked toward it. Upon arriving, she looked around for a container to lower into the well and saw a bucket. As she lowered the bucket into the well and looked down, it seemed like she was looking into forever, it was so deep.

When she raised it, to her surprise, it was not filled with water but instead, at the bottom lay a delicate sharply faceted diamond-like stone. She picked it out of the bucket and held it gently in her hand, awed by its stunning beauty. As she stood by the well, studying the stone, Lumina appeared to her.

Smiling she said, "With the sharp edge, slit a hole in the sky above you." The Woman looked at her as if she were crazy.

"How can I slit a hole in the sky?" she asked with a disbelieving tone of voice.

"Just do it" was all the answer she received.

Following the instructions of her mentor, The Woman raised her arm, the sharpest edge of the beautiful stone pointing straight up above her head. She stretched up as far as she could reach and with a slashing motion moved her hand across the sky. To her amazement, it slit like a scenery backdrop.

Lumina spoke. "You have made your first step in renting the Veil of Illusion that surrounds you. Now, climb up through it, and you will be on the other side of the Veil, where the beliefs start that create the physical world you live in."

The Woman put her hands on either side of the slit, and to her surprise she was able to lift herself up and through it. Getting her footing, she looked around, realizing that she was standing at a gate that opened onto a huge rickety hanging bridge that spanned across a seemingly bottomless chasm. She shivered as she thought of what might be next. Lumina stood with her at the entrance to the gate. "Below you is the Chasm of Doubt and Fear, and it crosses the Bridge of Limitations. If you have the courage to cross that bridge, you will travel a long way toward conquering your fears and releasing yourself from the limitations that now bind you. Mind you, in crossing the bridge you will confront many fears, and once you start across I will not be able to help you. You will be on that bridge and dealing with what each step brings until you get across. I can promise you that it is possible to cross it, and if you are persistent and trust, you will make it. Are you interested?"

The Woman was hesitant, but resigned. She knew that it was time for the task ahead of her, or she wouldn't be here, so she nodded her head and asked with trepidation, "Where do I find the key to unlock this gate?

"The key to opening the gate is Trust." Lumina explained. "Ask and you will receive, seek and you will find, knock and the door will be opened."

The Woman stepped up to the Gate and said, "I ask that I understand my limitations for what they are, so I can be free of them. I seek the understanding of how I created them, and I knock at this gate with the promise that it will be opened for me, allowing me to cross over this chasm of fear and doubt into a new reality. I demonstrate my trust by asking, my readiness by seeking, my desire by knocking."

The gate swung open as The Woman finished those last words, and she resolutely stepped out on the bridge, looking back to see that Lumina was gone, and she was alone. "She meant business," she thought to herself, "She isn't even going to stay and watch for moral support. What have I gotten myself into this time?" and she shuddered.

The Woman hesitantly started across the bridge. She had gone a short way when the bridge seemed to disappear, and she found herself about to step off into the deep chasm. She screamed in terror, and the edge of the bridge where she stood began to sway making her even more afraid. Her whole body was racked with spasms of fear rippling through her as she clung to what was left of the bridge.

"Trust, I must trust," she said making a huge effort to calm herself. "Lumina said I could make it across. I know I am ready to conquer my fears." As she said those words to herself, she was able to see the bridge again and resumed, taking each step slowly and cautiously. The bridge was very high and swung back and forth with every step she made. She was close to the middle, and the walking seemed easier, when all of a sudden the bridge ahead of her disappeared again, and the part of it where she was standing began to sway violently.

"Oh God," she cried in absolute terror. "I can't do this." As she said that, she could feel herself begin to slide toward the edge, and she felt helpless to stop it, until something in her snapped.

"Dammit, this is ridiculous," she yelled at the top of her lungs. "This is an illusion of my own making, why do I make things so hard?" As she said those words, the bridge became whole again, and she regained her footing. With a rush of adrenalin, she now felt much more confident and picked up her speed. She just wanted this to be over with. With that thought the bridge began to sway violently, as a piercing, icy cold wind suddenly began to blow across it. She groaned. This wasn't going to be over with so soon.

"What am I going to do?" she lamented, shivering with tears in her eyes. She pulled her cloak around her tightly, but was unable to hold onto it and the sides of the bridge as well.

"Here I stand at the brink of all my fears. My fears, my fears. What are my fears, besides the terror of the moment on this damn bridge?" she questioned herself standing there shivering and swaying in the wind. "What keeps me from moving beyond my limitations?"

She began to feel queasy. "Oh great," she muttered to herself. "If I get dizzy along with this nausea I'll really be in trouble!" She sat down on the bridge huddled tightly in her cloak, and shook with the cold and fear. She wouldn't be able to move farther across until she figured out what was holding her back. The swaying and her surfacing fears made the sick feeling worse. She was stuck and terrified.

She sobbed as her fears began to spill out, "I am afraid to be alone, I am afraid I can't make it financially, I am afraid of failing, dashed to pieces by my doubts and fears. I am afraid of the deep depression I can't seem to pull myself out of and the inertia it causes. I am angry at the thought of being trapped in this marriage that I cannot stand. I am afraid that if I stay with The Prince I will not be able to finish the journey that The Old One has promised I would make, and yet I am afraid of being alone. I am afraid that people will think I had failed, if I leave the marriage, and I am afraid of what it will do to my children. I am afraid to be without the Prince. I love him, and I hate him, and I don't trust him. I have hurt so much I am afraid to love, period. I can't go through all of that pain again. I am afraid of the pain that going through a divorce will cause. I am afraid of losing more of my children. I am afraid of living and afraid of dying. I am afraid of how I will feel if The Prince marries someone else. I have lived with him so long he is a part of me, even though it is a painful part. I am afraid of letting go of the pain because that is how I know I am alive!"

When she uttered those last words the wind stopped, the bridge stopped swaying and became a solid bridge, and she saw Lumina and the Old One waiting for her on the other side of the bridge which was now just a few steps away. She stood up, stunned by the realization of all her presumed limitations and their hold on her, as she had uttered them. She had faced her fears. She could see them clearly and realized that they were holding her in place.

Lumina and The Old One smiled at her as she finished crossing the bridge, and both of them hugged her in congratulations.

"Now that you realize how your fears have limited you, your process will be faster and reach deeper into the depths of who you are." the Old One explained.

"Now turn around and look at the bridge you have just crossed," Lumina directed. "It is now the bridge from idea to manifestation and is called the Bridge of Expansion. It crosses the Canyon of Probabilities. The River running through it is your River of Hope. There are many paths up the canyon to the bridge, and all of them are ripe with new possibility, which you will learn to bring into your reality."

As The Woman surveyed the vast panorama of possibility that lay before her in breathtaking splendor, she gasped with pleasure and wonder. What had been a scene of terror just moments ago now held a promising vision of possibility.

"Go ahead and try it out, make a wish," said the Old One. "Think of something you want to manifest and see what happens."

The Woman wished and found herself soaring over many probabilities, and she realized her world was full of choice. All she had to do was give up the fears that were holding her back, and she would soar. "I have had a taste of my real home," she whispered incredulously to herself, "and what a wondrous place it is."

The next thing she knew she was back in her chair in The Tower, and the depression had subsided. She was excited at the possibilities that lay ahead.

Soon after her experience with the bridge, The Prince made a comment to her that helped her see the dynamics between them in a much clearer way.

"It is a strange power you women have over men" he had said to her one day in an attempt to justify his actions. As she had suffered so much pain at the hands of men, she found his statement absurd. Now a new understanding began to dawn on her, and it had to do with projection and her relationship with the Prince.

Feminine Power

"I pondered what you said
Until it finally dawned on me
Why you seduce women
You think you take your power back!

In some strange way
You seem to know
That once hooked
A woman lets her feelings show
And she is brought into your rein
And you have your power again.
Women have the power to attract
But men ignite feeling in women
And we, gullible fools that we are
Give up our Power
And become emotional slaves
A container for driving needs.

All the while
Your excuse is "Feminine Power"
Instead of taking responsibility
for your pain causing deeds.

The Woman now realized that in the beginning of their marriage, she had projected her power onto the Prince, and he had projected his emotions onto her. So he became the Keeper of Their Power, and she became the Keeper of Their Emotions.

The Woman, now fully realizing how fear had kept her back began to assert herself in ways that she never had with the Prince. She began to write out some preliminary plans to help her see how she could manage apart from the Prince.

The Prince made the comment during this difficult time that he felt that he was losing control. Indeed!! She was bringing her projected power back inside of herself, and it made him uncomfortable because by bringing her power back, she in turn gave him his own emotions to deal with, and she was no longer protecting him from hers. With that profound realization she was able to see how those dynamics had played out in her marriage.

The Woman and her husband had arrived at an impasse. Their worlds were on two different paths, and those paths were not compatible to a marriage. Even though the transition would be difficult because there were still three children at home, they knew they had to separate, and they did.

The Woman sent a prayer up to Spirit.

Decision Prayer

Beloved Spirit,
I can no longer commit myself to my husband
I will no longer force myself
to stay in a marriage where trust is gone
I've been drawn into affairs
And used the excuse that since he had them
it was ok for me too.
I've rationalized about being unable to support myself
and about needing help with the children
And about the children needing their father
they do, but not this way!

I have prostituted myself on the bed of security
Full of fear, afraid to do this alone!
I am realizing this is a living death
which I can no longer endure!

This is my decision
I am committed
to travel alone
to the destiny
I was born to fulfill
I am committed
to following the impulses of my heart
trusting that they come from my Greater Self

I commit myself
to walking through the doors You open
to freeing myself from this marriage
I pray for Your Blessing and Guidance
as I step out into an unknown future.

Once the final decision to divorce was made, all the anger that The Woman had suppressed for years began to surface and erupted like a volcano within her.

She learned from Lumina that anger distances and was a necessary part of the process she was experiencing in order to come to terms with the destructive issues of the marriage and heal from them. Lumina's reassurance was little comfort, however.

Anger was very difficult for The Woman to accept in herself. Deeply ingrained in her was the belief that it wasn't proper for a woman to feel anger or express it. She felt so ashamed of her feelings and the hurtful thoughts that went with them. She wrestled with intense and frightening feelings and emotions that had taken on a life of their own.

For some reason she had been unable to express how she felt about anything to the Prince. Occasionally she would say something that he would really hear, but he had a way of brushing her off which diminished anything she said as irrelevant and unimportant. Now she was able to see how his attitude had kept her silent many times when it would have been healthier for her to voice her feelings.

She had always been so in control of her emotions, expressing them only when she felt comfortable in allowing them to show. Now there were times when she literally shook with the intensity of the explosive anger raging through her.

She prayed, she meditated, she journaled, she walked, she talked to friends but for awhile the harder she tried to handle her angry feelings the worse they became. She was embarrassed by the destructive and awful thoughts that came to her uninvited, goading her to get even for every injustice she felt he had ever dealt her.

She was beginning to understand the rage that drives people to murder, and she one day quipped to a friend, "It is a good thing murder is against the law!" and they both laughed, but she knew the feelings she had could be dangerous. For the first time in her life she was actually afraid of herself.

Years of repressed feelings were erupting with a vehemence that would not be stilled without help. The groundwork was being laid for a major turn in the road that lay ahead. Integrating her anger and the beliefs that had allowed layers of that anger to develop would require a teacher proficient in guiding her through some very difficult territory. Lumina sensed that she was getting ready and informed The Old One. He agreed and said he would herald the new teacher in a dream. It would happen in such a way that The Woman would know who was to be her new teacher. Meanwhile, she had one more piece of unfinished business to complete.

Altering Perspectives

The Woman had an opportunity to visit her eldest daughter who was living in the eastern part of the country where Ben was now living, and she knew it was time to see her old friend again. She was a bit apprehensive about seeing him, somewhat afraid of re-igniting old feelings that no longer tormented her, but her desire to see him overrode the apprehension, and she made arrangements to meet with him and spend the day.

Later in the evening, back at her daughters' home she went for a long walk on the beach and thought about the day and all that had transpired.

Thanksgiving Reflections 1985

I walked barefoot in the surf
the cold water rushing in and out
Playing around my feet
sifting the sand through my toes
and thought of you.

I remembered your face
that familiar dear smile
that used to make my heart race
as your eyes met mine
and as the fresh sea air kissed me
I remembered kissing you.

I reflected for a long time
watching the sea gulls and the surf
on all the feelings that rushed through me
when we were together
and how good it felt to hold you
if only briefly again.

I basked in the delicious warmth
of the sun
remembering the warm feeling
that always came through your eyes
and for awhile I remembered
just remembered.

My beloved friend,
you introduced me to my soul
for that I will always be grateful
but when you left for good
and I went so long without hearing from you
it hurt and
I felt as though my Soul had gone too
and for awhile I was very lost.

But my Soul, Bless it
Found me in the Tower
and comforted me
helping me to discover
places you could not
I realized all you could do
was show me the door, no more.

My Precious Friend
a projection of my Inner Teacher
for awhile
I know now
We are equal
travelers from the same womb
here to love and help each other

and through our experience
understand God better.

I watched a ship fade into the horizon
and thought of how afraid
I was to see you again.
Losing you was so hard
I didn't want the fire re-ignited
but I had to know.

I felt sad and relieved
Sad at the innocence we lost
relieved at the realizations I found
Deep joy at the connection
we will always have.

Please understand when I say
it felt so good not to need you
and still love you
and realize your part
in the journey of following my heart.
You became my teacher
and introduced me to my Soul.

Now, I'm becoming aware of my own power
following the path to my own destiny
I open my heart to the Universe
Breathe a silent prayer of thanks
for the important part you played.

The water laps around my feet
the sea gulls seem to hear my prayer
and the sun winks at me through the clouds.
They know.

Ben's open expression of his spiritual beliefs, his vast knowledge of the esoteric teachings that came from ancient Egypt, and his openness in sharing his knowledge and treasures with anyone who was interested had been a powerful aphrodisiac to The Woman. The Prince had made her feel foolish for what she wanted to learn and believe. Here was a man who was the embodiment of a model for a life she had yearned to live.

Now she was free to explore what she chose to explore, and Ben no longer had the same hold on her. She realized she loved the lore he shared about Egypt, but her own heart centered interests were different. She was more interested in human psychology as the path of evolution to spiritual development. She wanted to explore many belief systems, not just ancient Egyptian.

She was so grateful for that realization and understanding. She knew she would always love Ben, however, she was very comfortable with following her own path, and now she was sure it did not include Ben as a life partner.

The Woman had come to understand the part that Lord Sumina had played. He embodied the artistic creative drive that she had suppressed. His impact on her gave her permission to bring own artistic drive to life.

Life with the Prince had given her children which were the treasures of her life. She understood now that their joint contract was to produce the children.

She was finally able to accept that The Prince's main goal in life was to amass a fortune. He did. She was also able to see that the fortune he was driven to create was born out of insecurities caused by a very difficult and painful childhood. He had been abandoned by both parents and raised by relatives. His fortune seeking was his way of counteracting his insecurities caused by that abandonment. It was his security. She felt sad for him because in the process, he alienated most of the people in his life that wanted to love him and have a relationship with him.

Ironically, the very abandonment he had endured as a child, his children suffered because they felt emotionally abandoned by him. The Woman could see how he tried to control all of them with the power he thought he had through his money. He demonstrated to her the futility of trying to buy love. It only angered the ones that were being bought and caused tremendous resentment. She saw a misunderstood and lonely man who didn't understand himself either.

When she was finally able to feel compassion for the dilemma he had created for himself and see that all the destructive and painful events weren't really about her, but about ego patternings, childhood issues, and his own personal pain and insecurities, she was able to let go of him emotionally, and the anger left.

****

Amethyst took a deep breath and sighed as she thought back on these three men who had such a profound impact on her. The Prince had swept her off her feet as a young, naive maiden. With him she had experienced the raw, untamed feelings of first love, and she had become a wife and mother. As she began to really question her place in the world beyond family and motherhood, Ben came on the scene, and again she was swept away, this time intellectually. Ben took her to a deeper place in her own being, and she idealized him. Lord Sumina's influence on her helped her to begin to blossom creatively.

Now, so many years later she could see how each one had contributed to the development of a part of her. "Opening oneself up to love is such a double edged sword," she thought to herself. "If I had known from the beginning how much I would suffer, I wonder if I would have had the courage to allow it all to come to me" she mused.

It was twilight. The sun was reflecting its spectacular kaleidoscope of color on the water as it made another trip to the other side of the world. Amethyst sat looking out the window, drinking in the splendor. Life was so rich.

CONJUNCTION

"Conjunction is the empowerment of our true selves, the union of both the masculine and feminine sides of our personalities into a new belief system that must still be nurtured to survive. Conjunction can be seen as the creation of an intuitive "overself" and the achievement of what Carl Jung named Individuation."

The Emerald Tablet
Dennis William Hauck

A Seeker's Prayer

Reconcile me My Teacher
Restore me to your voice
Guide me in my thoughts and actions
Help me when I have a choice.

My desire is for your help
Your love I crave and need
I come to you Beloved One
Hoping I am worthy of Your Light
To fill me with your Presence.

I am ready for your instruction
I have nothing to hide
My mistakes are lessons
Hiding is caused by pride

You know me so well
Be gentle as you tell
Me my private hell
And guide me out.

I knock at the Door of Understanding
I seek your love and guidance
I ask for union
No longer separate but one.

I knock at the Door
I turn the knob, and wait
Praying for your gentle acceptance
And through the Work Of Life
And this Journey
Help me become One with You
My Greater Self.

CHAPTER NINE

LAZARIS

The Woman awoke one morning in early May from a dream in which she was reading a poem across the screen of her mind. In the dream it was Autumn, and she found herself in a park vibrant with vivid fall colors. Leaves were falling everywhere, and she was even aware of a breeze. She looked down at the ground and saw a square slab of stone with words inscribed on it. She stooped down and brushed the dirt and leaves off the stone and read the following inscription:

MY YEARS ARE SPENT
IN MIRACULOUS LIVING
A GIFT FROM THE DIVINE
OF UNCONDITIONAL GIVING.

The Woman sat up in bed and grabbed her journal to record what she had read on the stone before she could forget. She read the statement over several times, and thought about all of the painful experiences she had endured.

"Unconditional giving?" she exclaimed out loud to herself. "My whole life has seemed to be about conditions and my attempt to live with them and make some sense out of them! What a strange statement to dream."

She mused out loud, "this must a message from the Old One. He told me to pay attention to my dreams and said that he might send me messages this way. Well, this one certainly has my attention."

With that thought it seemed appropriate to pull a card in hopes that it would shed some light on the dream. She went to the Tower and took her beloved cards out of their hiding place. Unwrapping them, she said a silent prayer to her inner world for guidance, held the cards face down and pulled out THE HIEROPHANT.[1] As she sat there holding the card, concepts such as *teacher, following your intuition, learning to apply inner sacred teachings* floated into her awareness.

"Maybe this whole thing has something to do with this afternoon," she mused.

A friend had offered to bring a Lazaris Video over for her to see, and that was to occur later that afternoon.

****

The Woman was enchanted by what she saw and heard. The main message was that one creates their own reality through the beliefs they hold. Lazaris explained that personal belief systems generate a specific sequence of events which manifest the reality.

They explained that one's beliefs generate thoughts which elicit feelings. Those feelings produce an attitude upon which choices and decisions are made, and the reality is manifested. They illustrated how those steps become a loop that will continue to create the same reality over and over. Their explanation greatly expanded a concept that The Woman had heard many years ago *"Beliefs are like magnets, they attract events to one's life which perpetuate those beliefs."*

Lazaris made it very clear that if one does not consciously direct their personal reality, the unconscious and unexamined beliefs already set in motion during the initial programming of childhood would do the directing. They explained that life's issues would be lived and dealt with either consciously, by examining one's beliefs and changing them, or the beliefs would be brought to the surface through unconscious projection to be played out on the stage of everyday life. The way to change reality was to change the beliefs that drove the reality.

After the conceptual lecture which outlined secrets of success, Lazaris led viewers through a guided imagery to work with the material on a deeper level.

The imagery took The Woman deeper inside her own psyche than she had ever traveled before. After the meditation, Lazaris described several processing techniques in step by step detail giving the viewer powerful ways to work with the material that surfaced in the meditation.

The message was clearly about taking responsibility for one's life and issues, and the exercises in process and meditation were excellent tools to facilitate the inner work necessary to accomplish changes one wanted to make. Lazaris emphasized that in order to change one's reality, one must handle the beliefs and issues that were creating it. Once old beliefs were replaced by new ones then through the fuel of desire, imagination and expectancy one could change their reality.

The format of the lessons Lazaris taught was very similar to the format the facilitators used at the retreat The Woman had attended at Manna House, and she felt very comfortable with the process. The material Lazaris presented seemed to take what she was already learning to a much deeper level. She knew without a doubt that Lazaris was to be her next teacher. She had to study with this Entity.

The Woman had received a small settlement when she and her husband divorced. She reasoned that growing spiritually was the most important thing she could do for herself. *"Seek the Kingdom and the rest will be added unto you."* She made the decision to use whatever she needed of that money to do the necessary traveling she would have to do to study with Lazaris.

In the Autumn of that year, The Woman found herself in San Francisco at the first of many Lazaris seminars.

Lazaris used a specific format for their seminars. They introduced the subject for the day by discussing the intellectual elements. This was followed by a "blending" in which the participants are helped to feel a personal experience of the Lazaris Energy. More lecture, followed by several long and in-depth guided imageries each one building on the former one. These help participants to explore the deeper, unconscious components of the subject. They then give tools for working on an everyday level with what they have just learned.

Very early in the training, Lazaris stressed the importance of having a working relationship with the Higher Self and helped their students to develop that relationship. This was accomplished by taking participants into deep meditation, and through a specific initiation ceremony, the Higher Self would come to each individual.

At first The Woman's Higher Self appeared as a bright, luminous energy. Later after she became comfortable with this manifestation, Lazaris explained that it was helpful to be willing to have ones' Higher Self personify in some way, even though that was not necessarily their form. They explained that a personified Higher Self was easier to relate to while in a human body. A powerful initiation meditation followed.

It was at that time that The Woman's Higher Self appeared as a Native American Woman named Joriah. A close and intimate relationship quickly developed between the two.

The Woman had come to a phase in her journey that could be psychologically dangerous, but important territory she would need to travel. Lazaris instructed her that at all times when in deep meditation, which is where much of the work was accomplished, Joriah was to be there.

Lazaris explained that the archetypes she would be meeting and working with were very powerful and impartial energies, making no distinction or judgement about what they do. Lazaris stressed that it was important during this specific time to ask Joriah for permission before following any instructions from the archetypes, because it was Joriah who knew the territory and what The Woman needed for her development.

Most of the work that The Woman did with Joriah and Lazaris was in such deep meditation that she was not able to bring a detailed memory of the experiences back to the conscious state, but The Woman's conceptual foundation deepened considerably. The three years that followed were intense years for her as she grew in her ability to apply the principles and tools she learned from Lazaris to her everyday life. She felt herself shifting in profound ways, as her beliefs and perceptions of life continued to reorganize.

Lazaris helped their students to understand many of the ancient teachings on an intensely rich level seldom found in the modern world.

The Woman learned from Lazaris that she had been on Atlantis at the time of its' destruction. They explained that she and many others who were back at this time in the planet's history had participated in that destruction and had returned to help avert another disaster like the one that happened on Atlantis. This information added another piece to her puzzle of Ben's impact on her life. He too had been on Atlantis. He had been instrumental in getting her to start her search for her origins. Now it all made sense!!

She learned that she had also lived in Lemuria. Now she was being reintroduced to the Ancient Mysteries she had once learned on Lemuria, which included learning about her stellar origins and her purpose as a Mapmaker. (The name Lazaris gave the people doing this work.)

Although The Woman's inner life was rich and full of meaning, she couldn't help but feel impatient at the slower and more monotonous pace of her outer life. She comforted herself with the realization that the slower pace of her outer existence gave her the stability to travel to exotic inner places, but she couldn't help but long for her life to manifest more of the dreams she had seen in the world of probabilities. Her everyday life still left much to be desired.

So many of the events that had so drastically changed her life had been difficult and painful ones. Financially, life was much harder for her now that she was a single mother raising her children. Emotionally, she was lonely and yearned for a mutually loving relationship that would meet her on all levels.

Spiritually, she could see the truth in her life of the inscription on the stone in her dream. She had been given so much incredible information, and it had come to her during the hardest times when she felt the most guilty and unworthy. And dear Lazaris had come to her in the midst of all that difficulty, awakening her ability to dream again and to believe in herself enough to bring those dreams to fruition.

Now she was able to recognize many of her limiting beliefs and to understand the way those beliefs manifested her daily life, building her confidence far beyond anything she could have ever imagined in those years before she had met the Old One.

The Woman's most secret longing was to move away from the Plains of Reason. She had suffered so much emotionally on the Plains and yearned for the time when she could leave the memories and their reminders behind her. Her dream was to live nearer the ocean, which seemed like heaven to her compared to the Plains with their harsh winters and sweltering summers. She still had children in high school, and they wanted to finish their school years where they were established. She was committed to staying with them until they graduated and moved out on their own. After that she promised herself she would set out to create a new life in a new place. She focused on visualizing the goals for the future she desired to manifest.

In the meantime, she would continue to work to understand to the deepest level possible all the ways and reasons she created the reality she was currently in. She discovered that as she gleaned the gift of insight from each issue she processed, it lost its power over her, and she was able to let it go. Her insights were allowing her to forgive herself, a major step in learning to love herself. With self forgiveness came the realization that to the level that she could love and accept herself was the level she was able to love and accept others in her life. She could finally see that the giving of the Divine was unconditional, it was she who put the conditions on receiving by her beliefs. Plenty of work round her beliefs lay ahead, but she was encouraged by her continuing progress.

Sunny's Dream

"I see it in your eyes
I fear you will go away
I beg you to stay"
My child began to say

"There is white all around you

A beautiful hat you wear
A red and white dress
Your hands in a muff
Mother! You stare at me
You think I bluff?"

"A man dressed in black
I can't see his face
Comes to take you away
In a sleigh
A white horse to lead the way"

"Past a pond, through the snow
The horse pulls the sleigh
Where are you destined to go?
It puzzles me so!"

"I see two men, faceless and black
The horse slows down
The reigns begin to slack
You alight from the sled
Toward the two men you are led
There is a door ahead"

"A word Meorcole-El
It is a funny word on which I dwell
I fear death is in its spell
What is this story I tell?"

"You go through the door, mother dear
And now as a whirlwind you appear
Then I see you peering through a window
A baby sick inside She will live, you will die
Now the two become one and the child grows.

"And mother
These scenes are in your eyes
And around your head
They whirl continuously and
fill me with dread!
What could they mean?"

Amethyst read the poem she had written so long ago in an effort to try and make sense out of Sunny's dream and thought about her daughter in those awful days after Cherie's death. She was born a year and a half after Cherie and had never known life without her older sister. The sisters were very close, and in the aftermath of Cherie's death, Sunny had taken on a very difficult position. Sunny had experienced several foreboding dreams before Cherie's accident that pointed to someone dying. In those recurring dreams, Sunny dreamt that she had been shot in the back of the head while driving a car. Now Sunny was saying that it should have been her who died, and not her sister. Amethyst had sought counseling for her daughter in hopes of helping her see the situation differently, but nothing Amethyst or anyone else could say would convince her to think differently. She not only believed it was she who should have died, but had set a self-destructive course for herself. Amethyst was losing another child, and she didn't know how to stop it or what to do.

It had been shortly after Amethyst began working with Lazaris, when Sunny had the strange dream. She had gone to her mother deeply troubled and related the dream to her.

The dream had such stark images in it, and the name Meorcole-El sounded mysterious and yet familiar in some strange way. To have Sunny dreaming another dream of death was very frightening to Amethyst.

Amethyst thought about how ambivalent she had become about her life during that time and remembered how part of her fear was in tandem with her own desire for escape. Her inner life had become much richer, as she gained proficiency at putting her losses into perspective. At the same time she was aware of the sharp contrast between the progress she was making and her children who were still grieving hopelessly. The task of helping them seemed like an insurmountable job. Dealing with her own pain had taken so much of her energy, and now Sunny's dream reminded her once again of the comfortless place her children were still in.

Amethyst took a deep breath and began to write. She hoped she could put into words the extraordinary occurrence which was born from the anguish of that episode...

CHAPTER TEN

THE MAGICIAN'S GARDEN

It was a cold winter night. The Woman sat in her chair in front of the fireplace musing about how often it was by the winter's radiant fire where her most profound discoveries seemed to originate. She loved to watch the fire, forever fascinated by its ability to completely transform anything it came in contact with. She watched the flames lick around the logs releasing vivid oranges and blues and reds, continually changing patterns of light and color accompanied by occasional crackels, snaps and hisses. "The fire is so alive, almost like it had a personality of its own," she whispered to herself.

Tonight, as she gazed at the flames she puzzled over the images of Sunny's dream. She was holding her beloved cards, hoping they would give her some help. Whispering a prayer for guidance, she reached into the deck and pulled out THE MAGICIAN.[1] She sighed. She didn't feel very magical tonight, only weary and discouraged. She held the card though, and waited. She had asked for guidance, so this had to be the correct card.

Soon she felt a gray mist surrounding her, and everything began to take on the now familiar timeless feeling. She stood up and walked over to the window, and as she looked out over the snowy landscape, surrounded by the mist, she instantly knew what the dream was about.

I look out over the landscape of frozen passion
A silent reminder of potential untapped
Covered by a layer of cold white snow of dormant possibilities.

A sleigh is ready to carry me away
A driver, dressed in black is coming to meet me
The coachman stands, ready to greet me

Dressed in a gown of white, trimmed in red
I depart
eager to go
reluctant to start.

The magnificent white horse
Prances through the snow
The air is brisk
I feel such a glow

But
A feeling gnaws at my gut
The sleigh doesn't make a rut!
Two men have no expression
No face!!
The world is turning black at a fast pace!

A whirling feeling surrounds my Being
I move toward the figures waiting
I'm cringing.

A door Meorcoli El I'm beckoned through
I ponder I waver I know not what to do!
Hesitantly, I pass through the door
Knowing I as I am will be no more
Whirling, sparkling energy I become
And the door shuts on another one.

What is the meaning of this?
The feeling utter bliss
Fear is gone, and I know I exist!

"Greetings, I am Meorcoli-El the Magician" he said, as she found herself reforming in a garden. "Congratulations. You have found your way to the Garden of Desire that exists below the frozen landscape of your life. It is here that all the seeds of desire that you have planted in your lifetime lay dormant, waiting for you. Through your work here you will bring spring to the frozen terrain you traveled over to get here.

This is a unique garden." he went on to explain. "It continues to come into existence as you discover it and all of it is a part of you."

With those words, he motioned for her to follow him. Feeling somewhat disoriented, she struggled to keep up with him through a thicket of untamed bushes with a small path cut through. Finally, they arrived at a marble temple, with beds of beautiful flowers planted in the gardens that surrounded it. She stood there a few moments, catching her breath. No matter how many times she journeyed with the Archetypes, she was surprised and in utter awe of the situation she found herself in. This time was no exception.

The Magician motioned her to follow him, and they went inside, entering a spacious open room, with large columns of glistening white marble supporting the roof. Large ornate alcoves graced the four corners of the room. In the alcoves were huge vases filled with flowers. The vases in the north and south corners were full of the most magnificent red roses she had ever seen. In the east and west corners the vases bloomed with elegant bouquets of white six pointed lilies.

Meorcole-el directed The Woman to a small altar in the middle of this large open room. On the altar were four objects a wand, a sword, a chalice, and a coin. As soon as The Woman arrived in front of the altar, Joriah appeared. The two women hugged in happy greeting.

"Welcome," she said. "I have come to join Meorcole-el and together we will be giving you a very important initiation."

The three of them turned to face the altar. The Magician stepped out in front of The Woman and Joriah and faced them as he began to speak in a solemn tone. The Woman felt a shiver through her body, a premonition of something very significant about to take place.

"These are the tools of manifestation you will need to cultivate your Garden of Desire so the seeds of your chosen destiny will take root and grow."

Merocole-el reached over and picked up the long wand with his right hand and held it up toward the sky.

"This wand represents focused will. In pointing it upward you recognize that all power comes from a greater part of yourself and not the small ego self you are most familiar with. The wand symbolizes the Fires of Transformation. Never forget where your power comes from. When you use this wand, you acknowledge that your human self is a channel for your Greater Self. This wand corresponds with the element fire and the Archangel Michael."

With those words he handed the wand to Joriah who took the wand, turned to face The Woman and touched the top of her head. The Woman felt a rippling vibration in the crown of her head as a vibrant energy illuminated her head.

Joriah then handed the wand to The Woman and instructed her to stand with the wand in her hand just as Meorcole-el had demonstrated. The Woman took the wand from Joriah's hand, turned toward The Magician and raised it above her head as he had done. As she did, she felt the flow of the energy in her head cascade through her, illuminating and warming her body. She then laid the wand carefully on the altar as she was instructed to do.

Next, Meorcole-el picked up the sword.

"This sword is the Double Edged Sword of Discernment. It serves to remind us that our thoughts and actions create and destroy. Through the process represented by this sword your world is changed. For every beginning something must end, and for every ending something new will begin. Use discernment in your actions and remember you must respect the power you emanate, for it is rapidly increasing! Be impeccable in the choice of words you speak, and mindful of the possible consequences of the changes you pray for. Remember, you are responsible for the intent in the words you speak. This sword corresponds with the element air and the Archangel Raphael."

He handed the sword to Joriah, and she touched each of The Woman's shoulders with the sword. Joriah then, very carefully touched The Woman in the middle of the forehead with the tip of the sword. As the tip of the sword touched her forehead, The Woman felt a disorienting and reordering of her thoughts and a profound realization of the power her thoughts and words possessed. She became very weak and dizzy and felt as though she might faint.

Joriah moved the sword away from The Woman, allowed her to regain her balance, and then handed her the sword to hold. Joriah explained that she needed to hold the sword until she absorbed the energy emanating from it. She shook as she struggled to hold the sword, then something in her shifted, and she felt a strengthening move through her being. When the vibrations stopped and her legs felt stronger, she stood up, walked to the altar and carefully laid the sword on the altar. The realizations it imparted to her continued to swirl around in her consciousness for a long while. Joriah and The Magician waited patiently until she indicated that she was ready to proceed.

The Chalice was made of polished silver and was carved with figures of the Moon in all of its phases. Meorcole-el held it up with both of his hands as he said, "Drink of the Waters of Feeling and Emotion drawn from the River of Hope. By drinking of the same waters, we share your emotional experiences which helps us guide you. Know that your feelings strongly enhance the power of your thoughts and actions and will intensify the power of all that you seek to manifest. Emotion is a powerful force which drives your actions. Observe your own process. Be aware of how your actions follow your most powerful feelings and remember you are responsible for those actions. This Chalice corresponds to the element water and the Archangel Gabriel."

He then sipped from the cup and handed it to Joriah, who also took a sip. She then handed the Chalice to The Woman, and she sipped the liquid in the cup. As she swallowed the deliciously sweet liquid, she felt her body undulate with emotion. Every cell tingled with a delicate and bittersweet feeling. The emotions pulsating through her body caused her eyes to brim with tears. She was overcome with a deep compassion and love for her children, and then the feeling spread out to include the people of the world and the gamut of human emotions. She had never experienced anything that felt quite so poignantly profound. She placed the Chalice back on the Altar. Her whole being continued to reverberate with the intensity of the human emotional state.

The Magician picked up the coin, the final object on the Altar and held it between his hands charging it with energy. Then he handed it to Joriah. She too charged it and handed it to The Woman. The Magician spoke: "This coin represents the abundance of the universe, now at your disposal. Mind you, it always was, but you have to be willing to receive it for it to become available to you. By both of us putting a charge on it, we agree to inspire and help you to become multidimensionally prosperous. We cannot make you prosperous, but we can inspire you and guide you to understandings which will open up channels now currently closed because of your beliefs. Here is a hint. Study your beliefs around prosperity, your deservability of receiving, and your willingness to allow. Lazaris will also help you with this. This coin corresponds to the element earth and the Archangel Uriel."

As The Woman held the coin in her hand, she immediately understood that money itself was a neutral tool. She received a powerful knowing that abundance was a birthright, but her willingness to receive it and her belief in her deservability about receiving it were large factors in how much abundance she would allow herself to have. Some realizations about a contract or agreement to explore the limitations around abundance began to surface. She was able to understand that working against the limitations of lack had helped her to develop strength and creativity. This concept piqued her curiosity, and she vowed silently to herself to explore this issue further. She laid the coin back on the altar in its rightful place. The tools were now a part of her.

The Magician began to speak.

"You have just received the Initiation of Abundant Manifestation. You are being guided to transmute your personal world, and as it changes like the ripple in a still pond, shifts will happen in the world around you as well. You are now entrusted with the knowledge of these powerful tools. They are the tools you need to fulfill your destiny. You are no longer the person you were when you arrived in this place. An old part of you, the sick baby in Sunny's dream has transcended into the new life being born in you at this moment.

"Together with these tools and your desire, imagination and expectancy you can learn to create anything you choose. This is the true power of Magick. You have at your disposal the help of the universe for you are a part it. The Archangels corresponding to the elements I just explained are also available to guide you through inspiration.

"Magick happens when you realize that you are in a dream. The physical world of manifestation is a dream. Once you fully understand that truth you can be awake in the dream. When you are awake in the dream, you can make the dream come out any way you chose, because you are the dreamer."

Joriah continued, "One more thing needs to be clarified. You are learning to be a co-creator. To be effective, it is crucial that you understand the difference between expectation and expectancy.

"For example, say you want to create something. You imagine it very precisely, you have a strong desire for it, and you expect it to happen. At this point you must drop the control of how it will happen and allow it to unfold in its own time and way. Know it will happen (the expectancy) without controlling the process (expectation).

"Remember that you have many inner friends available to help you. In the physical realm, you cannot be aware of all that happens on the inner planes to bring your dreams to fruition. That is why it is so important to state your desire, your dream as clearly and precisely as you can and then let go of it and let us go to work. Tell us what you want and need, and we will do what is necessary to bring it to you at the proper time."

Meorcole-El then spoke to The Woman, "Another piece of this sweet mystery is this Awareness is the ability to recognize the Mystery in all of creation. The cards you use to beckon us are a part of that Mystery. They hold Memory.

Each letter, each number, each picture has a special meaning and reason for existing, it is all a code. You are relearning what was lost to you by your work here, and in the process you are reclaiming the code. What you are doing is a part of your chosen destiny. The fact that you are here with us, is a sign of a level of growth and commitment to this Way.

"Keep in mind that your children are just as powerful as you, and they are guided too. They have experiences to stimulate their growth, just as you do. Your transformation is helping them, even though you don't think you are accomplishing much now. They are blessed because of the work that you do. I know it is hard for you to understand, but you are receiving blessings from them as well. From their cues, you search and grow in your effort to help them. You see how interactive the drama is from the bigger picture? Remember you all shared in the creation of this dream. Deep in their unconscious they too know what you are bringing to conscious awareness, for you are all deeply connected. In all your interactions with them let your love for them be your regulator, and you will guide them with what you are learning. Don't try to directly teach them this unsolicited, just answer any questions they ask truthfully. They will seek and discover their path on their own, in their appropriate time. Be an example through your own healing and growth, and they will take from you what they need" Joriah comforted The Woman.

"May I ask you just one question?" The Woman said.

"Of course," they both responded in unison.

"Well," she said hesitantly, "I am so concerned about Sunny. She has it in her head that she should have been the one to die, and nothing I or anyone else says seems to have any impact. I am very worried about her. What can I do to help her?"

The Magician answered gently, "It sounds like she has allowed herself to be overcome with what your world calls 'survivor's guilt.' I am not at liberty to tell you everything, but suffice it to say that she and Cherie may have a past life karmic connection. Along with that, she is experiencing emotions that for her purposes in the bigger picture of her own cosmic drama are important experiences for her to have. Keep in mind that she is a spiritual being in her own right, here to explore certain tracks of experience and emotion. Cherie's death put her on a track that she will have to come to terms with herself. Your development has a good chance of helping her and that could be a part of your contract with her. Continue to present to her avenues of discovery and help, and she will take what speaks to her. Keep in mind that on the deepest levels a great deal of sharing and healing are exchanged. Keep up with your work and surround her with your loving light as your commitment to her. At present she is caught in her own matrix of belief systems and prior contracts which direct her impulses.

"Bathing one you wish to help in a bubble of loving light is a very powerful technique for aiding someone. Help on the inner planes as I suggested is very powerful and will have impact, because all are ultimately destined to heal. If you ponder what I have just said, I think you will grow into a deeper understanding of her dynamics and your relationship with her."

The Magician smiled at her, the expression on his face comforting her while at the same time telling her the session was complete. Joriah hugged The Woman and in that precious moment she knew she was deeply loved and that her children would ultimately be ok.

The Magician saluted her with a bow.

"I am always here, ready to make Magick when you are" he said with a grin and a wink.

The next thing The Woman knew, she was sitting in her chair by the fire, "THE MAGICIAN" card in her hand.

DISTILLATION

"Distillation consists of a variety of introspective techniques that attempt to raise the content of the psyche to the highest level possible...Distillation takes us into the rarefied realm of the One Mind...It is the purification of the unborn Self all that we truly are and can be spiritually."

The Emerald Tablet
Dennis William Hauck

CHAPTER ELEVEN
REALIZING SYNERGY

Several months went by, The Woman continuing to work with her inner teachers, Joriah, Lumina, the Magician and Lazaris. Guided by her beloved friends, she spent a great deal of time writing in her journal, reading books, and meditating. Integrating all that she was learning was hard work, but gave her life so much meaning she thought of little else.

She was beginning to understand herself on several levels and had started to have subjective experiences of the Divine Feminine Energy. These experiences led her to see that a deep pervasive sense of shame gnawed at her core of self-acceptance. This shame had penetrated her entire world view and was linked with growing up with the notion that because she was female she was somehow "less than" a male.

The Woman had questioned her belief in the Male God of her milieu for many years, especially after she had left the church organization that was so rigid. She was beginning to realize, however, that remnants of those teachings she had been taught to believe as a child and young adult still lingered. She had questioned for years the validity of teachings about a God who was an avenging, all powerful, get even, jealous God, who at the same time was supposed to be a "God of Love."

She could not see how a God that was supposed to be all "Love" could be all those other things too. She resented the story of Adam and Eve and the idea that God could punish a whole gender because one ate a piece of forbidden fruit. It just didn't make sense to her that an all knowing God of Love could be that petty.

She was incensed by the attitude the world held that little girls and women were there for men to use and abuse. She resented the teaching that women were the property of males.

The Prince held on strongly to that belief, even after they had left the church, and it became one of the nails driven into the coffin of her dead marriage to the Prince.

When she confronted the Imago of her step-father at Manna House and released the repressed episodes of abuse out of their hiding place, all the shame that had been buried with it had begun to surface. In tandem with the surfacing of the shame was a gnawing anger that smoldered just beneath the surface of her awareness.

It was fortuitous that during this time The Woman made the decision to go to college. Her discoveries at Manna House awakened in her a fascination with the world of Human Psychology, and she knew this was the area she wanted to study.

Through her studies, The Woman was led to see the progression of historical events from which the western world's paradigm of beliefs had evolved. She learned that the world view held by current thinkers and philosophers made a huge shift into the age of the Scientific and Industrial Revolution starting in the sixteenth and seventeenth centuries. The belief in an organic, living, spiritual universe was replaced by the belief in the world as a machine to be dominated and controlled.

As the Industrial Revolution gained more of a stronghold, a polarization took place. The Scientific and Industrial Revolution looked at Nature as inferior, Science as superior. Nature was labeled feminine, and Science was viewed as a masculine discipline. Science was determined to dominate nature, so naturally masculine determined to dominate the feminine.

Profound realizations about the development and power of belief systems began to form within The Woman as she learned that the influences which shaped the scientific world view were well over three hundred years old. She learned that the stage had been set for this polarization long before the scientific world view became the paradigm of choice in the western world. She read that as far back as Aristotle, women, sex, nature, the body and emotions were seen as inferior. Males, the mind, a life of reason were seen as the superior path.

The book *THE TURNING POINT* by Fritzof Capra[1] spoke deeply to The Woman. She came across a quote by Sir Francis Bacon which illustrated graphically to her the thinking of the paradigm that had so powerfully changed the world view. According to Capra, Bacon and others like him radically changed the nature and purpose of the scientific quest. Until their time the goal of science had been to understand the laws of nature and live in harmony with them.

Since Bacon, the goal of science had become one of to learning to dominate and control nature. His advocated method of investigating Nature stated that *"Nature has to be hounded in her wandering, bound in service and made slave."* The aim of the scientist was to *"torture nature's secrets from her." "His view of nature as female whose secrets have to be tortured from her with the help of mechanical devices is strongly suggestive of the widespread torture of women in the witch trials of the early seventeenth century." (THE TURNING POINT p. 56)*

It was becoming clear to The Woman how the Mechanistic World View had begun to sound the death knell to the ecological survival of the planet, by stripping humans of their deepest creative process (which comes from the feminine principle) and the planet of Her resources by disrupting the delicate balance between organisms.

She discovered that the early Church's plan to gain control through obedience and devotion, attempted to divorce the expression of love and devotion from sexuality by teaching that human love and sexual experiences belonged to the lower or animal instincts.

The atrocities of the Inquisition focused on usurping the hold the Goddess centered religions had on its followers. The Goddess religions revered all of nature for its life giving abilities as gifts from the Goddess. In order to bring the Male dominated church into power, reverence for the Goddess and all things female had to be destroyed. This gave men a license to mistreat women, as they could blame their sexual attraction to women on their lower animal nature. Women were desired and at the same time seen as an evil influence on their "higher spiritual" aspirations. Women could be branded as witches, sorceresses, and enchantresses taking the male away from the devotion to his god and his church. This thinking divorced sexual expression from love and acceptance, turning male and female relationships into a love/hate viscious cycle, and sex into a moral issue.

In this way church and state could claim the devotion of loyalty, and the expression of sexuality became stripped of its deepest meanings, creating a paradigm of dominance and submission.

The Woman was enraged and sickened to see how these beliefs had been propagated through time, and dug destructively deep into the core of many facets of life in the western world.

She felt compassion for so many families caught up in this paradigm of beliefs which was deeply destructive to couples trying to love each other and the children they were raising.

Her compassion finally transferred to her own situation as she realized how those beliefs had worn away at her own marriage, ultimately playing a part in its destruction. Straining under the burden of all the repressed rage she held, she had projected her anger at being subjugated by the male gender onto The Prince.

She could see how men who put themselves on a "better than" ego trip in their relationships with women did themselves a grave disservice as part of the human family.

"Oppressors are robbed of their ability to develop the deepest of spiritual qualities because a premise of self-righteousness and superiority keeps one on a superficial level of understanding.," she wrote in one of her papers. *"The creative gifts and drives of women who suffer under this dominance, relegated to the level of second class citizens and forced to struggle with the oppression of low-self esteem and low self worth are lost to the world forever. The ramifications of having virtually one-half of the population based on gender alone struggling with these issues, and the shame they*

produce creates a tormented society which continues to perpetuate unnecessary pain, and incredible loss of human creativity and development.'2

The Woman discovered some important clues to the differences in the way male and female perceived life when she began studying the concepts of right and left brain theory. The theory taught that wholistic awareness was a right brain function, while the left brain was focused and linear. More pieces of the puzzle fell together as she explored the belief that female expression was typically right brain dominant and male expression typically left brain. This could explain somewhat how males became dominant if they had a more developed ability to focus on ideas and bring them to linear manifestation, step by step. However, if the right brain is where the ideas and creativity originate, then it too is needed and important. Hmm. Lots to think about.

"How sad that an entire gender is disregarded because they were not being adequately taught to access the left brained ability to focus their ideas and creativity, not to mention the rote left brained learning that squelched a great deal of creativity in both genders" she mused.

Now The Woman could see how this lie had been perpetuated that championed the belief in only a male god, and the disservice to humankind it wrought. Disregarding the idea of a feminine side of god was a disservice to all who believed that way. Women were left without a Divine Counterpart to relate to and made to feel like second class citizens. In order for women to <u>feel</u> truly equal to men, they must be able to recognize themselves in God, for humans were told that they were created in God's image. She reasoned that it was not anymore psychologically healthy for a man to feel superior, than it was for a woman to feel inferior. Now, understanding the concept of projection, she wondered if maybe humanity had projected human characteristics onto God and created God in man's image. The Woman struggled with these concepts and pondered them deeply.

In this state of contemplation, The Woman knew it was time to visit the Tower once again. She needed to talk to someone, and she knew the best guidance would be from one of her Mysterious Friends. She would only be allowed two more draws from the deck, but this was important, and she knew it was time for guidance from an Archetype.

Shuffling through the cards on this quiet, starry night she made the decision not to pick a card, but to let her Inner Friends do it for her. The Woman said a prayer to her Friends, turned the deck over so she couldn't see what she was drawing and reached in and pulled out a card called "THE EMPRESS.[3]" She held it, noticing that the figure looked pregnant. She was struck by the beauty and power that emanated from the figure on the card. She wore a crown of 12 golden stars on her head. She held a shield with a dove on it in her right hand and a sceptre in her left. She sat on a throne in a field of wheat, and her left foot rested on a crescent moon. Everything about her spoke of beauty and power and fertile femininity.

The next thing she knew The Woman found herself sitting on a barge in the middle of a beautiful crystal clear lake. A thick mist hovered over the lake. The barge seemed to be floating toward the shore barely visible off the distant horizon.

She found herself dressed in a long green dress of the most exquisite soft and delicate material that shimmered and rustled softly with her every movement.

The barge floated onto the shore. The Woman was met by a much younger woman dressed in a long, elegantly cut velvet bergundy dress. The younger woman curtsied to The Woman and greeted her. "I am Garnet, Guardian of the Lake" she said. "Welcome to the Land of Creative Imagination. You have arrived on the shores of the Island of our Beloved Empress, Esmerelda. She awaits your arrival. Follow me please."

The Woman felt elegant and regal in her attire and moved as though she were floating up a long narrow road. She could barely see the silhouette of a castle in the foggy distance. Finally, they arrived at the drawbridge to the entrance to the castle. It was down and waiting for them. They walked across the long drawbridge, past some guards.

Garnet spoke to them in a language The Woman did not understand. They smiled and motioned for her to proceed. Garnet called to the Guardians of the Door, and the magnificent wooden doors slowly opened enough to let them through. They walked across a huge cobblestone courtyard to a large building and stepped inside a massive domed foyer. Straight ahead of them was a large, ornate wooden door, with carvings on it similar to the images on the card she had pulled. A guard standing by the door opened the door, and Garnet motioned for The Woman to go inside. She instructed her to walk up the long royal blue carpet until she reached the part in the carpet where it turned deep indigo. At that point she was to bow low and stay there until Her Highness told her what to do next.

The Woman followed Garnet's instructions and bowed low before the Empress when she reached the Indigo color in the carpet.

"Beloved Daughter, welcome, I am so glad you have come." Esmerelda began speaking as she stood up and motioned to The Woman to do the same. "Your ponderings and searchings have led you to pierce the Veil of Oppression that hides many secrets of your gender from you and your sisters. Congratulations! Your tenacity has won out. It is time for you to learn of a great truth."

She clapped her hands three times, and Joriah and Lumina appeared from somewhere behind Esmerelda's throne. After joyfully greeting her two friends, Her Highness led them over to a long stone slab that filled one corner of the throne room. It was covered by a deep purple down filled velvet mat and had a golden cashmere shawl draped over it. The Empress motioned for The Woman to lay down on the mat. She sunk down into the soft down as it cuddled around her body making her feel warm and secure. The Empress covered her with the golden shawl.

"This is truly a momentous occasion," said Joriah. "We have the pleasure of bestowing upon you The Initiation of Synergy."

Joriah took her position at The Woman's head, Lumina stood at her feet, and The Empress stood by her left side. A large rose quartz crystal was placed on the The Woman's abdomen, and a clear quartz crystal was pressed up against her feet by Lumina. Joriah placed a Moonstone on her forehead, an amethyst at her crown, and The Empress positioned a diamond cut emerald on her heart.

The Empress began to speak:

"These crystals and gems hold a remembrance of energy within them of your history. Through this initiation we will implant this memory back into your present body. Are you willing for this information to be given to you at this time?" The Woman firmly stated "yes I am."

The Empress said some words in a language The Woman did not understand, and almost instantly, she felt a surge of energy from the crystals pulsate through her body. The pulsation increased in intensity until her body started visibly shaking. At that moment she experienced the sensation of growing larger and larger until she became Diffuse Awareness, and in that instant, a gestalt of understanding took place in her consciousness. As the gestalt permeated her consciousness, she heard The Empress's words drifting to her through the expanded state of awareness:

"In the beginning was Diffuse Awareness. It was all, it was everywhere. It existed without form, it simply was. It existed for unknown eons in that state. At some point in Its existence, It became aware of a longing within Itself for something was missing. It was very lonely and suffered from A Great Cosmic Boredom for It knew all and was all. Out of that loneliness a great longing arose in Diffuse Awareness causing great turbulence, and Active Awareness came into being. Active Awareness had the ability to focus Diffuse Awareness, and Creativity was born. Creativity caused great tension between Active Awareness and Diffuse Awareness, and Polarities became a dynamic in the expression of consciousness as a result of this event. Together, Diffuse Awareness and Active Awareness set out to create Galaxies, by infusing holographic fragments of Themselves into their manifestations through Creativity.

Over aeons, however, the Dynamic of Polarity caused the holographic fragments to polarize, expressing the energy of either Diffuse Awareness or Active Awareness forgetting the other existed. Different galaxies and planets expressed varying degrees of harmony, depending on whether or not they remembered that they were a complete holograph of Diffuse Awareness and Active Awareness or not. For the most part the fragments polarized and expressed as one or the other.

"Long, Long ago, in our present Galaxy, far away beyond the realm of time and space as you know it, a fragment of polarized Active Awareness whose name was Yin, became acutely aware of a longing within itself for something was missing. Its longing was so intense that it sent out a magnetic wave of attraction that was felt by a fragment of polarized Diffuse Awareness at the same level of longing and awareness. This fragment's name was Yang. The Law of Attraction drew them together. When they met, a shock was felt throughout the Galaxy, for at that moment the Polarities of Yin and Yang came together for the first time within our Galaxy, and a synergistic field of consciousness came into existence.

"The powerful Synergy of these two Polarities of Consciousness meeting created a longing for a multitude of expressions, the next step in Their development. The idea began to materialize of finding a place where Synergy could play and experience Themselves in many forms.

"Synergy sent out a search throughout the Galaxy looking for a planet which held the vibration for thought to become form. Soon, they discovered that a planet named Gaia had been born that held great promise. It's vibrational level was just what was needed for the Grand Experiment of Synergy. Gaia was a planet that had been born to hold space and mark time.

"Synergy visited the planet and found that Gaia indeed had great potential for development. Synergy asked the planet for permission to bring Its Consciousness as form to live on the planet. Being a young planet, it was very flattered to be chosen for such an exciting mission and readily agreed to this Grand Experiment.

"Now Synergy in the Formless State was very harmonious, each Polarity enchanted by theOther's Characteristics. They were able to come together in a way that what They were together was far more than what They were separately, and yet They maintained their individual characteristics. It was only natural that each wanted to create so they discussed it and made the decision to each design images like they imagined themselves to be in form. They would create all forms to be physically compatible counterparts to each other, as They were consciousness counterparts to each other. In this way They could experience Themselves in countless ways, which promised to expand Their experience of each other considerably.

"Gaia was prepared. Yang brought the sun, the light, the active energy, the heat, the day, the summer, the masculine form, and the energy of expansion. Yin brought the night, the moon, the passive energy, the cold, the winter, the female form, and the energy of contraction. With the gifts of Yin and Yang, the Seasons were born, the play of day and night began their eternal dance, and Synergy began its journey on Gaia.

"Yin and Yang were enchanted by the forms each designed for the other."

The Woman's consciousness was spinning with visions of the profound realizations she was beginning to grasp. It was becoming clear to her that the Feminine Spirit was an expression of being, and the Masculine Spirit was the expression of doing. She realized where the world had the idea of a Male God, because Active Awareness is easier to identify. It Acts. It manifests, but the Feminine held the creative potential from which Action drew upon to manifest. The Feminine was the original energy!! And yet in that moment she KNEW there was no separation. One cannot exist without the other. All humans were a combination of Diffuse and Focused/Active Awareness Synergy God and Goddess and their offspring a manifestation of Creativity.

In the instant that she realized that there was no separation, her eyes opened, and she was lying on the slab, nestled in the soft down once more. This time however, a male figure was standing beside The Empress.

"I wish for you to meet my beloved," The Empress said. "It is He who brings order and manifestation to all that I hold as potential. The world could not exist without the work we both do. Every Being that lives on Gaia carries within them the pattern of Empress and Emperor[1] God and Goddess Diffuse Awareness and Action."

"Now I can take you deeper into this secret veiled multidimensional mystery," Esmerelda went on to explain. "We hold the original human form pattern for Yin and Yang the Counterparts of The Great Synergy who created male and female in your world. Yin is Diffuse Awareness. She holds potential for all of creation. Very simply put, She gathers to create form as one gathers thread to weave a tapestry. Yang as Focused or Active Awareness creates form to manifest content, as in setting a goal and using the form of the goal to encourage its manifestation.

"Each human on Gaia holds the pattern of Synergy. As male or female you have split them into outer and inner, but they really do not exist separately.

"Remember Animus? He is the subconscious, or inner Yang form for your outer, consciously feminine Yin. For men it is simply reversed: Yang is the outer form, and Yin is the Anima or unconscious inner form. Every Being on this planet is a hologram of both Diffuse Awareness and Active Awareness, an image of Synergy.

"One of the major tasks of your journey has been the process of discovering this mystery and learning of your own completeness. As you grow in awareness, you become more able to utilize both the masculine and feminine energies, and your life becomes more balanced and harmonious."

The Woman said. "Something puzzles me. Gaia is in trouble, and the manifestations have become so destructive, what is that all about?"

The Emperor nodded his head as he said, "It is unfortunate that Gaia has become unbalanced, and that is where our story continues." With those words, he touched each one of the stones on The Woman, and again a surge of energy went through her body, and another gestalt of understanding began its descent into her field of consciousness as The Emperor spoke:

"At first, life on Gaia was harmonious as Consciousness played with form, creating new forms and discarding old ones, experimenting with perfecting and developing form. Aeons passed, it is not known exactly how long, but Synergy and the inhabitants on Gaia became bored with their experiment.

"It was all very fun to bounce in and out of physical form at will, but there was no edge to it, no challenge. They had total power, in and out of the body, and everything always turned out as expected. A discussion was held by Synergy and their offspring and the decision was made to up the ante.

Now that they were proficient in moving from physical life to consciousness and back again, they would be given choice to make the game more interesting. The choice would be to be allowed to forget their Celestial Origins while inhabiting a body. This would be accomplished by stepping down their consciousness. A small fragment of consciousness they named ego would now inhabit the body, and be its caretaker. It would be such a minute fragment of the Complete Essence that it would not be able to remember its origins. The Essence, unknown to the ego fragment, would stay in constant contact with the ego. Because the ego could not remember its origins, Essence would discover just how much could be learned by the smallest fragment of consciousness on its own. This posed an interesting question. How small a fragment of the whole could learn and create and develop? It was postulated that as the ego fragment learned and developed, more and more of the Essence could join the ego in the body, eventually spiritualizing the physical form and coming back to the original plan, but with a deeper knowledge, experience and development of physical life.

"They speculated that this would make life on Gaia more challenging and interesting, and the experiment would be valuable. In physical form, the descendents of Synergy would have to draw upon their human resources to meet the challenges on Gaia. It was hoped that the inhabitants of Gaia would develop more abilities and skills without the memory of their origins as a safety net. The tension to develop and survive would stimulate a much stronger creative drive.

"All who lived on the planet would be given the choice to be subject to this rule. The decision would be made before they were to be born into a body, and the forgetting was usually complete by the time a child was six years old.

"Two safety clauses were set-up. There was a group who chose from the very beginning of this experiment not to forget, so the memory of their celestial origin would always be available on Gaia when an inhabitant was ready to remember. They were called The Rememberers and could communicate telepathically with all beings on Gaia.

"When the longing to remember began to awaken in someone, the longing would send out a certain vibrational frequency which The Rememberers were sensitive to. This guaranteed that when One Who Had Chosen To Forget began to look for its origin, the Rememberers would begin to work with them to help bring them back to their original status.

"The fragments of consciousness of all the inhabitants on Gaia would visit the Synergistic Plane during the deepest part of sleep at night. In this way their psyches would stay connected to their origins even if they did not remember while on Gaia. If they became ready during a given lifetime to remember, the impulses to search would begin coming through from the sleep state into the waking reality which would set out the vibrational signal to The Rememberers.

"Synergy would not intervene, but allow each form to make choices about how they would live on Gaia, and She became known as The Planet of Choice. Coupled with Choice would be a creation of a life from the beliefs that sprang out of the choice. The beliefs would allow the consciousness to experiment with a lifetime immersed in the belief system of choice. Ultimately, that meant that each being on Gaia basically lived in his/her own world of beliefs. All perceptions would perpetuate the choice made, and an inhabitant would build a life by stringing perceptions together to match the original choice.

"It was not long before power struggles began to develop between Yin and Yang in their many forms. The planet that was once a playground, became a battlefield. Synergy and its offspring did not take into consideration the power of polarities on Gaia without memory of its origins. Fear split the ego consciousness into a positive and negative ego. While the positive ego cared for the body and grew in its creative ability, the negative ego became consumed by fear. To compensate for that fear, power became the most important drive. Now each inhabitant on Gaia had an internal war going on inside, as the positive and negative egos struggled with the life circumstances they found themselves in. With so many beings at war with themselves, it naturally resulted in wars between peoples as they polarized in their belief systems and tried to make others believe as they did.

"Still being born into body after body, but forgetting that they could move beyond the physical form, or access help from their Greater Self, they became fearful of the discarding of that form which now was labeled 'death.'

"Fear and Power became the dominating forces on Gaia, as the veils of belief became thicker and thicker. Even though the fragments went back to the Synergistic plane at night, fear kept the impulses of remembering from coming through to the physical vehicle inhabited by the ego because the egos were so stuck in their limiting belief systems. Over time the forgetting became almost complete. Life and death, now the most powerful polarities of all, held Gaia's inhabitants to a wheel of life after life and death after death, and death became more and more of a fear.

"Whatever issues were not let go of when one left the body in death were imprinted in an overlay upon the energy field of the infant when it was born into the next body. Even though the belief system might change, the issue would manifest in some way in the new life until it was dealt with and no longer held a charge on the consciousness. Each new life would create new issues, keeping the consciousness ever on the wheel, with no way to escape.

The call to the Rememberers was getting less and less until only a few Rememberers were left, and they were forced to stay hidden. The knowledge of the Rememberers was in danger of being destroyed.

"Darkness, once revered as a time of retreat and rejuvenation, a time of deep learning as consciousness returned to Synergy while the form slept, now became a time of dread and danger. Light, once treasured as the time of activity and creativity, now became a time of enslavement, and most of the inhabitants of Gaia lost the feeling of joy and exploration that first brought Consciousness to play on the planet.

"Not all is lost, however. Synergy is learning of the power of polarities at the most mundane level. The anxious tension of dread plaguing mankind has indeed stimulated tremendous learning and inventions.

"Now, the inhabitants of Gaia have developed technology which enables them to learn more and more deeply through science how it all fits together, and the process has the potential to bring humankind back to Synergy. Synergy and Gaia together are ready to move into another Spiral of Evolution, a new paradigm of discovery. As the new paradigm begins to manifest to a greater degree, it is hoped that Gaia will once again be brought into balance, and Synergy as an equal dynamic of forces will be once again honored and manifest.

"This was the choice of manifestation Synergy chose at the beginning. Both male and female are equal and belong together in harmony. Part of the destiny of you and others like you are here to accomplish is to help bring back the balance of Yin and Yang into form. If this is accomplished as hoped, the promised world of peace and joy will be a reality upon Gaia.

"You responded to the impulses of your deepest Self and brought yourself to this place where you are now allowed to take part in the birthing of this new paradigm. This is the reason you were born at this time. The decision to take this journey had to be of your own free will. Congratulations, you have come a long way."

The Woman was overwhelmed with gratitude and awe, her head swimming with the realizations of all she been taught on the Isle of the Empress. Never in her wildest dreams did she believe her searching could bring her to such an amazing explanation of life.

"Hold this information as sacred" Joriah said to The Woman, and held out her hand. The Woman sat up and took her hand. She bowed very low before both the Emperor and Empress in deep respect. Each in turn hugged her. Tears of gratitude and emotion filled The Woman's eyes.

Reluctantly she turned to leave the chamber with Joriah, who led The Woman back to the barge. They hugged, and The Woman stepped reluctantly back onto the barge. She did not want to leave this magical place.

Creative Imagination
The Empress

My Beloved Empress
Pregnant with the world of form
Beautiful in your creative fullness
Waiting for your idea to be born.

Impregnated with the Seed of Thought
From the thrust of my imagination
You nurture and grow an event brought
Forth from the Womb of Creation.

Heavy with the inertia of fullness
Labor will soon begin
The Force of Destruction constructing
Things will never be the same again.

A labor is never easy
Regardless of how deep the desire may be
To Bring forth an idea from creation
Here for the world to see.

To bring forth this seed from my being
From thought to active event
This period of gestation
Must be time well spent.

I nourish it with education
Building concepts, watching it grow
It is becoming so full inside me
I find myself longing for it so.

But it must not come prematurely
This labor must start at the right time
This work to bring to fruition
The sum of all my intuition
A labor with order kept in mind.

I prepare once again for labor
For I have labored before
In awe of the force which propels it
I relax, prepared to open the door.

In the beginning it all seems so easy
It's misleading, I soon become queasy
As it progresses and I know it won't stop
So much is happening, I'm shocked!!

My life will be so different
With this idea in physical form
A times I'll wonder if it's worth it
Should this idea ever have been born?

The first few months of worry
As the fragile infant takes form
Are fraught with doubt,
And fear that it will come to harm.

but once its existence is established
Then joy in my creation sets in
It will develop and be successful
And it is on to creating again!!

CHAPTER TWELVE

RECONCILING FATHER

After her experience with THE EMPEROR and THE EMPRESS and learning the Story of Synergy, The Woman began in earnest to focus her work on reconciling and healing her deep seated feelings of animosity towards men.

She had been separated from the Prince almost five years before she had allowed herself to respond to that old familiar feeling of attraction toward men who came into her life.

She was still somewhat wary of them, but one of her lifelong goals was to be in a relationship that met her on all levels. She had a taste of what that might be like when Ben and Lord Sumina were in her life. She had been working hard on her issues, and she felt ready to love again.

A man came into her life who was several years younger than she was and had three young children who had barely started school. She was so intensely attracted to this man, as he said he was to her, that it surprised them both.

At first, she had strong reservations about joining her life with someone with young children, hers were nearly through high school, but soon she was falling head over heels in love with him. Caught up in the intensity of her feelings, she rationalized that maybe it wouldn't be so bad raising more children. His children were very sweet, and they adored him as he did them. The Woman was especially enchanted with the way he interacted with his children.

There was an undercurrent of unspoken tension however. Both of them had reservations about the relationship they were reluctant to share with each other, each afraid of breaking the romantic bubble they were caught up in. The reservations intensified the romantic tension, infusing the relationship with a sad yearning that neither of them could put into words, but soon began to erode at the core of their attachment to each other.

Peter had recently separated from his wife and was very devoted to their children. Whenever his ex-wife wanted him to keep the children he was right there. Nothing mattered more to him than than time spent with his children. He was reluctant include The Woman when he was with his children, and he would sometimes break dates with her to be with them. This puzzled and concerned her, and she began to question him about what part he wanted her to play in his life. Her questions irritated him. He wanted to be with her, but couldn't understand why she didn't understand his need to be with his children and their need for him. He later admitted to her that he was also struggling with his reservations about their age difference and the contrast between the ages of his children and hers.

The Woman became more and more anxious and depressed as the old familiar feelings of mistrust and the fear of rejection clouded her thinking. She could not trust his word, and her anxiousness grew. At the same time that she was hanging on tenaciously to the relationship she was wrestling with the question of why he meant so much to her. He was treating her very shabbily, but he wouldn't come right out and talk about his feelings. He was saying that he wanted the relationship, yet The Woman was feeling something entirely different from him.

It was in this state of emotional turmoil that The Woman made arrangements to go to spend the weekend working with Lazaris, who was conducting a seminar in a town a few hours drive from where she lived.

The Woman settled into the first meditation of the weekend. Lazaris took them through the process of relaxing and letting go that always whisked her off into the deepest parts of her inner world.

She began sinking deeper and deeper into blackness. As she felt herself sinking and floating, she became aware of herself as a child of around three years old. She lost all awareness of herself as an adult, she was the three year old child whose father had left her, sobbing inconsolably with grief and rage at being abandoned and the heartbreak of losing her father.

During her early childhood years, The Woman lived with her mother, brother and maternal grandparents in the same house. They had come to live with her grandparents after her mother separated from her father. Her grandmother hated her father and would say terrible things about him. He had betrayed her mother, and therefore the family, and there was no reconciling the angry bitterness they felt toward him, even for the sake of his two children. The children were told he was an awful man, not worthy of being loved, and they were not encouraged to have any kind of relationship with him, or feelings for him.

The Woman's grandmother had a great deal of power within the family structure. She helped The Woman's mother in many ways, and she understood at a very young age that her mother and brother and herself would not survive without grandma's help. She was very grateful for all that her grandparents had done to help them, and she was also very afraid of her grandmother's wrath. Grandmother meant security to her as a small child. She learned very quickly that she was not to do anything to threaten that security.

Within this emotional dynamic, the little girl formed an intense loyalty toward her grandmother and a deep shame for being the offspring of this man who had treated her grandmother and mother so terribly. She was about four when her parents separated. She never saw him again except for a few times when she was around five or six. Because of the shame she was made to feel and her loyalty toward her mother and grandmother, she repressed all of the feelings of love she had held for her father, as well as the sorrow of losing him and worked very hard at hating him.

With Lazaris' help she plunged into the rage the child within her had harbored at being abandoned. She sobbed the grief and pain of all those years of her childhood she had spent missing her father and wondering what was wrong with her that he did not love her enough to be there for her and fight for a relationship with her.

Immersed in this experience, she finally understood where a major part of her deep yearning and melancholy nature originated. She wore a heavy blanket of shame and grief that had become the core around which she had constructed her emotional self. The hatred she tried so hard to develop toward her father to deflect her grief and shame

146

eroded away at her own feelings of self worth and cast a gray hue of mistrust over her perceptions of the men in her life.

In the midst of this gut wrenching ordeal, it dawned on her what hold Peter had on her. Here was a man who loved his children enough to fight for them and was an excellent father to them. The children were allowed to see him and be with him.

The wounded small child inside The Woman wanted him to be her father her too. She had transferred the love that she had repressed for her father to Peter. There was her old friend Projection showing its' smug face again!

The Woman cried and cried for hours, releasing all the pent up fear of abandonment, grief and insecurity she had buried deep inside her, surfacing every time she got into a relationship with a man. She now realized that the deep seated fear of being abandoned was part of the core of her failed relationship with the Prince, and one of the reasons she could not trust him. He had suffered abandonment by both of his parents and had been raised by an aunt and his grandfather. Now she could see the whole setup! They brought similar issues to the marriage and mirrored them to each other. He couldn't trust her either. It was a marriage doomed to fail.

She also recognized another dynamic that had woven itself into her attractions to other men during her marriage that contributed to her being drawn into affairs.

The Woman had grown up with a gnawing ache on the periphery of her emotions taunting her with the thought that "somewhere out there was a man who 'really' loved her." Now she realized she had projected lost father into the outer world, and it produced men who would take up parts of the projection. Keeping the unconscious pattern in place, they eventually abandoned her, continuing the dynamic. It all made sense now!! This influence had been a major pattern in her dealings with men.

She realized by the end of the weekend that she had reached and released a core issue.

The Woman and Peter went their separate ways soon after she returned from her weekend retreat.

"I realize now what a gift Peter was to me," she wrote in her journal. "It was through loving him, and the circumstances around my fear of losing him, and the anguish that caused, that I was finally able to reach the core of the pain I have always carried."

The melancholy demeanor left, and The Woman now experienced a lightness and sense of freedom unlike anything she had ever before felt in her life.

Within a year after she and Peter parted, a man was to walk into The Woman's life who would not only change her life completely, but become her life mate.

****

It was raining hard, one of those rains in Northern California where it feels like the ocean has turned upside down and just let go, pouring itself out onto the land. The surf pounded against the shore, dashing hard against some the rocky cliffs further down on the beach, creating a distant rhythmic roar. The frogs chimed in their peculiar song, adding joyful croaking to the ensemble of this stormy night. Inside the fire sparked and crackled, casting a reddish orange dancing hue over the room. Hugh sat at his keyboard, his music blending and enhancing Nature's Orchestra. Immersed in this rich kaleidoscope of sound, Amethyst had begun her evenings' writing. Now finished, she sat back, closed her eyes and allowed herself to be carried off by the rhythms of her surroundings.

Soon, new realizations began to surface, bringing another angle to her awareness of the deep shame around her sexuality that had been so much a part of her as she grew into puberty.

Sometime in those adolescent years, she had become obsessed with being accepted by God. She now saw how she had constellated all her issues of forced hatred for her father, his abandonment, rejection and the subsequent shame, along with the shame from the abuse she later suffered into a core belief that there was something very wrong with her. To compensate for those terrible feelings of not being good enough, she had created a Persona that struggled to be perfect. She strived to be everything to everyone, trying so hard to prove to herself and the world that she was indeed acceptable.

At the same time, she harbored a deep seated anger at God, who had let all those things happen to her. Then there was the issue of being female and acutely aware of the undercurrent attitude toward her gender of "not being as good as" the male gender. Being mad at God was unacceptable of course and to compensate for those feelings, she did everything she could to try and appease God.

She could now see how as a child she had been a victim of the adults who were supposed to be responsible for her while she was small and vulnerable and unable to be responsible for herself. Diety didn't need or want her appeasement, only for her to accept herself and willingly receive the gifts that life had to offer.

Tears began to trickle down her cheeks as it dawned on her that her whole life's quest had revolved around proving to God that she was indeed acceptable. She could see it all now so clearly, as she put the story into words. She had discovered just how cherished and loved she was. She had been imprisoned by belief systems. She didn't have to appease God or anyone, or justify her existence. Her existence was its own glorious justification.

The sound of the rain cleared the air, synchronized with Amethyst's falling tears washing her soul clean, as she let the deepest and most pervasive layer of separation go.

Ready To Leap

Now, as The Fool
I stand on the Brink
Of a new frontier,
An uncharted course
Ready to leap into my new world.

I reflect one last time
On the journey
That has brought me this far
Knowing the leap will set my past free.

I reminisce with feelings of deep gratitude
For all the help I received from my Friends,
The Old One, Lazaris
My Higher Self, and the Archetypes
Loving Beings from another world
Eager to show me The Way

Beloved Old One
First to greet me from the Inner Planes
Ever present and loving Guide
Readying me for journeys into wonder
Encouraging me to delve deeper
Not content with superficial explanations
You challenged me to probe
For things are not always as they seem.

I utter a poignant sigh
Remembering inconsolable tears and bitter farewells
As I stumbled in the Abyss of Grief
Battling the Dragons of Guilt
By the Sea of Desperation
Tossed upon the Rocks of Anguish
Deep in the Storm of the Tempest.

Where weak and exhausted
Begging to die
In the midst of the nightmare
They heard my cry!

Lazaris
You helped me find my wings
And gave me reason to soar
You encouraged me to believe in myself
You loved me
And showed me
The world I had yearned for
In some forgotten dream

You brought me to my Higher Self
And taught us to communicate
The two of you showed me possibilities
Beyond my wildest imaginings!

Through a Voice
And a Spark of Light
You patiently and lovingly guided me
To the realization
It was all a dream
A myth
A labyrinth of illusion
I'd created for myself
To travel upon and explore!

With love and peace
You opened the badly healed wounds
And cleaned out the festering sores
Then with your love
You showed me how to heal them
This time leaving no scars!
And in your gentle and caring way
You taught me how to dream again!

In deep gratitude
For all that I feel
I grope for the words to describe
An indescribable wonder of self
So intense
It is orgasmic in its exquisiteness
Making me feel so alive
Every cell tingles with the knowing!!

And now
As The Woman
On the brink of a whole new world
Empowered by the knowing of the Synergy of Myself
I call to my world
In a voice filled with love and gratitude
"I am free, I am free"
And the voice echoes back to me
A sound of sheer ecstasy
And I laugh!!

It was all my own making
A tragic, melodramatic play
In which I've played all the parts
Victim, tyrant, martyr, mother, daughter
Sister, wife, lover.

I've been rejected, betrayed
Abused, so confused
Running the gamut of painful emotions
Scattered with fragments of the hints of love
And what it might be

Until finally
Sick of the suffering
Letting go of the fear
It is finally clear!!

I am ready to love
For the fear of pain

Has lost its power over me
I am Free
To create my own reality!!

I AM and it is passionate!
I AM -and it is good!
I AM and it is so right!
IAM and it is love!
IAM free!! I AM Me!!

CHAPTER THIRTEEN

THE WORLD

Amethyst sat writing at her desk. It was a balmy, clear evening, and she had the windows open so she could hear the soothing sounds of the surf. She leaned back in her chair, starring at the computer screen and breathed a deep sigh. A feeling of elation shivered through her as she typed those last words, "I am free, I am Me!"

She sat thinking about the tapestry of gestalts she had woven with the threads of her story. She had planned to end her story with that poem, but somehow it didn't seem complete. Something was still missing, she thought to herself as she looked up at the full moon illuminating the waves, casting its shimmering path on the water.

It suddenly occurred to her that The Woman had not drawn the eleventh card. It had not been needed in the story to the point that she had taken it, but now she felt some very strong urgings to do it, and she knew it was time. Now far into the future from the time she lived her life as The Woman, Amethyst would draw the last card.

A chill of apprehension. shuddered through her as she put the cards face down and uttered a prayer to be guided to the most appropriate card. She reached into the deck and pulled out THE WORLD.[1]

She sat back in her chair and gazed at THE WORLD card in her hand. Lulled by the rhythm of the surf, as it continued in its interminable journey to the shore and back to the deep again, she sat contemplating the card, wondering what it could possibly have in store for her.

She soon became aware of a cloaked figure walking down the moonlit beach toward her. A joyful cry of recognition leaped from her mouth as she realized The Old One was walking toward her. At the same time, almost as if she had walked down the moon path on the water, Joriah joined The Old One, and now here they were, coming up the walk to her door together. She opened it, joyfully hugging each of them as they walked through the door.

"Dearest One," began The Old One, "tonight's writing is a testimony to how far you have come! It has been an honor to work with you and guide you to this moment. With the pulling of the last card your fate is sealed. Within the journey of the cards you drew you were given the opportunity to grow and develop. You have accomplished that task far beyond anything we had hoped for. In the process you have shifted your consciousness into a new paradigm. In that paradigm we are no longer needed in our current form."

Amethyst felt a cold chill go through her, as The Old One spoke. There was a tone in his voice she had never heard before, and it made her uncomfortable.

"It is appropriate that you hold THE WORLD card in your hand," he went on. "With the realization that you create your world and your willingness to take responsibility for it, you have become a part of a new Order. As you leap into your new world, you will no longer be under the influence and guidance of the Archetypes of the Old Order. Our job was to assist in bringing you to this place and realization. Now you and others like you, have become an Archtype a prototype of a new way of thinking which is emerging within your culture.

"Soon you will meet with many others with whom your story and journey resonate. You will all be sharing your personal stories and seeing the similarities and patterns, and together you have the chance to make the New Order a manifest reality.

"From what we can see at this time, there are many on the planet who are working for a world that is ecologically balanced; where male and female are recognized as equals and encouraged for the talent they have, not the gender they are. They can envision a world where many Paths are honored and recognized for the truth they hold, and where prejudice is just an isolated incident not the mindset of the milieu. We see a culture emerging where superficial religion has lost its grip because a deepening spirituality has grown in importance. From those visions many changes in the world have the potential to take place.

"We see this world on the horizon and feel fairly confident of its manifestation. At the same time, there will be resistance from the Shadow of those who still have a great deal of darkness to deal with in their own lives. You have experienced in your own life how powerful Shadow's projection is. It will emerge in full force and cause great anguish in its resistance to the New Paradigm. Many people realize that change is necessary, but more are afraid of change. You can see for yourself the struggle you went through to create the changes in your life and understand your own shadow impulses.

"It is necessary for you to remain strong in order to witness and not become polarized over these events. Keep uppermost in your mind that a new order is working to assert itself. The trouble will come from the clash of the old and new paradigms and is inevitable. The Good News is that it isn't the end of the world, as many have thought, but the end of the world being driven by unconscious forces. In the New Paradigm, it will be the responsibility of the world's inhabitants to work things out through conscious decisions. We watch, we wait, we hope."

Tears began to roll down Amethysts' cheeks. She loved The Old One so much. Parting with the Old One was not at all what she expected as her "reward" for all her work.

"I and the others represented by the cards belong to the journey of the Old Paradigm when the teachings had to be in secret. This is no longer the case. The teachings will be coming out in the open more and more now, and the content will be greatly expanded. That will be one of your jobs in the New Paradigm. The time of secrets and hidden meanings is over. Take your place beside those who have also arrived at this juncture and do not worry my child, you will still have all the help you need. All you will have to do is go into your inner core and ask. I will be watching you and cheering you on, as you feel your way in the new world. Be of good cheer, for your work has released us too. We are soon to discover what our job in the New Order will be. Who knows how or where we will meet again, but I am sure we will. Now, it is time for us to say good bye."

He hugged her, and before she had time to protest, with a wink and a bow, his image began to fade and he was gone. Joriah held Amethyst as she wept and comforted her until her sobs subsided.

"Parting is hard," Joriah said. "Just remember The Old One will always live in your heart in the teachings and guidance he has given you. You know nothing is ever gone forever. You have given him a wonderful gift by the work that you have accomplished. Now that you are no longer subject to the unconscious projections of the Archetypal Energies, you have freed him and the rest of them to go into the New Paradigm in another form."

"Your work has helped to bring a paradigm of unconscious energies into conscious realization. You have reached a level of growth within the New Order where you are ready to consciously create your life. You have become a co-creator. For all those in the New Paradigm, the Old World is finished. This is what the old prophets foresaw. Not the end of the world, but the end of the world created by unconscious forces. The new world cannot be prophesied because you and others like you will create it. The future, The World, is indeed in your hands."

Joriah went on, "and now I have a gift to give you and an Initiation. I will now tell you our story from my vantage point."

CHAPTER FOURTEEN

REMNANTS FROM THE FIRE

Amethyst closed the windows against the chilly night air. One of the features she loved the most about living near the ocean was the way it always cooled off at night, making sleep deep and restful. However, now the room had gotten quite chilly, and it would not be comfortable to stay there without a fire.

"Would you mind if we waited until I can build a fire before you go on?" Amethyst asked.

"Go ahead and start the fire," Joriah encouraged her. "I have a lot to tell you tonight and we may as well be comfortable."

Amethyst began the process of building the fire with the logs she had placed on the hearth earlier that evening before she had begun to write. As soon as the fire began to burn steadily, she left it to put some water on for tea. Now the two women sat in the chairs in front of the fireplace with their tea and some biscotti she had baked earlier that day, and Joriah began:

"Aeons ago, you and I were one. It is hard to describe how we were one, while you are in human form, because there are no words to adequately portray how it works. Suffice it to say that we were. We were a part of a Great Whole that longed to experience Itself in an entirely different way, even aeons before the meeting of Synergy and the idea of the Grand Experiment was conceived. There were many levels of division of the Great Whole before the longing and meeting of Yin and Yang brought about the Grand Experiment on Gaia.

"Each Essence who wanted to participate in the Grand Experiment of physical life, which meant inhabiting a body on Gaia agreed to split apart, one part inhabiting the body, the other part staying behind in order to guide and help the part that became physical. It was thought that much could be learned by doing this."

"You remember the story of how Synergy came to live on Gaia?" Joriah asked. Amethyst nodded.

"There is another chapter in that story as it pertains to you. I am pleased to tell you that you are ready to learn of the Plan of Grace.

"The Rememberers were called 'The Wise Ones' 'The Old Ones,' and 'The Masters.' Through the ages the Rememberers worked hard to keep the original teachings safe. They traveled the Galaxy where Synergy dwelt, learning and teaching. They remembered the love that existed when the Grand Experiment first started, and they felt deep sadness for all who were lost on the planet.

"Over the Aeons they devised many ways of perpetuating the Sacred Information as well as protecting it. When it was safe to do so, they maintained Mystery Schools for those ready to begin the journey home.

"During the very dark time in Gaia's history when the inhabitants of Gaia's forgetfulness was so complete that the planet was ruled by doctrines of separation and fear, the information became gravely endangered. A plan had to be devised to keep the information available for seekers and concealed at the same time.

"One of the methods used for keeping the information alive and safe was the development of picture cards depicting the journey home. To someone unaware of the memories, the cards were no more than pretty picture cards; but to one seeking to remember, the pictures on the cards could awaken the archetypal energy within the psyche of the Seeker. The Remembers could then guide the secret work as it unfolded. The Old One explained that to you in the very beginning. But there is more.

"Gaia has grown tired of the Grand Experiment. At first during the harmonious time, She thrived and was able to stay in balance. As the power struggles between Yin and Yang grew more vicious and fear ruled the inhabitants, the energies of Gaia were thrown completely out of balance. The cold became colder, the heat hotter, and many lifeforms started dying because of the ecological imbalances. Gaia began losing patience because as the offspring of Synergy had walked the planet, She too has been learning. She remembers how good it felt to be in balance, and she grieves over the lifeforms she can no longer sustain.

"Gaia has grown angrier and angrier at Synergy for all that has been inflicted upon her. She thrived on the balance of Yin and Yang, she agonizes and writhes in pain from the imbalances forced on her Being. She has grown disgusted and repulsed by the apparitions of fear spread in the ethers surrounding her. This disgust and repulsion has caused such great distress that it is disrupting Gaia's weather patterns causing great suffering for all.

"Synergy and the Wise Ones do not know how much longer Gaia can endure the injustices forced upon her, and the suffering of Synergy's offspring is getting out of hand. Belief systems of destruction and violence and power as domination have overtaken the planet.

"Gaia holds a resonance in the Galaxy that would be hard to duplicate, and Beings from many Galaxies are putting pressure on Synergy to do something. They do not want to lose Her because She is so dear to all that know Her. There are other problems as well.

"Once Consciousness arrives on Her soil, they are reluctant to leave, and now the forgetting is so complete more and more offspring are returning through the wheel of rebirth, and Gaia is overloaded. She cannot maintain life at the current pace indefinitely.

The wealth of the planet is distributed very unevenly. A small portion of the planet's inhabitants are in possession of most of the wealth, while a disproportionately large number of people on Gaia are living in inhumane poverty. This is causing exponential imbalances. All natural systems, ecological, animal life, and planet resources, as well as human endeavors are distressed by this disharmony, causing humans to be afflicted in a multitude of ways, intellectually, physically, emotionally and spiritually.

"A new plan had to be devised to save Gaia and return the offspring of Synergy to the remembrance of who they are in order to bring harmony back to the planet.

"Gaia has proved through her loyalty and cooperation with Synergy that she is worthy of ascending to a higher, less dense vibration. The Era of the Grand Experiment is almost over. A new way of being on Gaia has to come into existence that does not include separation as it is presently experienced.

'Synergy has discovered that It can ascend to a higher vibration and degree of unity, if It can bring Itself together. The Grand Experiment has served its purpose.

"Several generations ago, as you mark time on Gaia, the call went out for Volunteers, and a Great Gathering was held. Synergy and all the Remembers as well as the Higher Selves of the Seekers, and the Wise Ones, the Old Ones and the Masters were present.

"Something had to be done to help Gaia. A plan had to be devised which would encourage the inhabitants of Gaia to make the choice to succeed. Synergy has unwittingly been caught in a trap of its own making by appointing choice, through the dance of polarities to be the operating law of the planet. Force will not solve the problem and cannot be used because of the law of choice.

"This mission is as important as it is dangerous, because of the seductive resonance now inundating the planet. Now it is so easy to forget the reason for being on the planet that extra precautions have to be taken even to ensure the success of the volunteers.

"All volunteers for this special mission have to either be one of the Rememberers or a Seeker who has spent several successive lifetimes on the path of Awakening. The Higher Selves were appointed to be the ones who made the decision of whether or not a Seeker was advanced enough to be of use to the mission.

"It was decided that The Seekers who were ready for the mission would carry an implant in their minds which their Higher Selves would administer at birth. It would begin transmitting information to the Seekers at the time when the attempt would be made to make the Great Transition back to a world of remembering on Gaia.

"Working with the Seekers was going to be tricky. They were ones already on the path of Awakening, but they were still working out their own imbedded belief systems, which included fear as a major obstacle. They continued to have the choice of how fast they would work to undo the impact of lifetimes of entrenched forgetfulness on Gaia.

"It was decreed by Synergy that any Seeker who of their own free will chose to accelerate their Awakening during this exceptional time would be given a special dispensation of Grace. Grace would enable them to work and release faster than the old ways of lifetimes of study.

"Once the Seeker had made the conscious choice of their own volition to awaken, then the Plan of Grace was immediately bestowed upon that Seeker. The plan waived the rule of choice once the the Seeker made the commitment. It was possible to waive the rule of choice, because any Seeker who was able to understand their life issues beyond the binding energies of the polarities would be advanced enough to realize that the only choice they had was to bounce back and forth between polarities. Once a seeker moves beyond the polarities a different way of thinking manifests within the person, and choice looses its attraction. Then the Higher Self could take charge and make decisions from a much more expanded vantage point.

"It was arranged for available Seekers to be born into the middle of the century in order for their hoped awakening to coincide with the projected vibrational shifts on Gaia close to the end of the century. It was important that they be mature enough to deal with the situations that would present themselves when the shifts began to happen.

'The Rememberers would be around as they always were and accelerate their search and instruction of all who were ready to be a part of the new plan.

"Teachers who specialized in the nature of Consciousness were sought out to be available from all parts of the Galaxy to speak through some of the Volunteers who chose to be channels for these teachers."

"There were many other kinds of jobs available for the Volunteers to choose from. Some would write stories that would trigger memories and/or the desire to help. Others would act as guardians, protecting the volunteers and inspiring them at times of crucial decisions.Others would simply live quietly and hold a healing resonance in the collective unconsciousness. Many of the Seekers would be born into difficult family conditions that would stimulate them to want to pursue psychological healing of those conditions. This was crucial, for each person that healed a major issue plaguing a family would set a healing resonance within the psychic field of the family and contribute to the healing of many generations.

"Others would work directly with Gaia to try and re-establish the balance that had been lost. They would study ecology, work to clean up toxic waste, become vocal and catalystic in saving natural resources and endangered species of animals.

"In the Psyches of the Volunteers tremendous shifts had to happen for the Awakening to occur successfully. A Volunteer had to start life on Gaia in a normal way and live with the issues of the family they were born into, as well as the initial forgetting in early childhood. They were not exempt from working out the belief systems they had set in motion for themselves in their current lifetime, or had brought from a former lifetime. They would need to have a current and remembered experience of the human condition in order to create the massive shifts they had volunteered to help with.

"You see, your body is a projection of consciousness, a probe or conduit if you will. A very small fragment of consciousness inhabits the body and downsteps to the frequency of its surroundings. In order for true healing to take place, the frequencies have to be raised from the inside out. As you work on an issue and resolve it, you literally bring 'light' to the cells, healing the cells and erasing the cellular memory of the issue. Your body pulsates in syncronicity with Gaia's pulse. As you bring light to your cells, you pass it on to Gaia, where it is absorbed into the morphogenic field, literally breaking up paradigms of beliefs.

"The initial animating energy stepped down into the physical vehicle is easy for the ego to deal with, because humankind has been doing it for thousands of years. What we are trying to do now is raise the frequency of the physical body and of Gaia. That requires more energy than your body is accustomed to accepting. Being blocked by limiting beliefs and energy sapping issues keeps the frequency low. As healing and expansion take place, the release of the blockage in the cells creates a space, an opening for light to enter, and the frequency can be raised, allowing a higher vibration from your Greater Self to enter the physical body.

Because the body is made of materials from the body of Gaia, anything that affects the body affects the planet. In this way the energy is anchored into Gaia. Anchoring the higher frequency into Gaia also assists her in her development to the next level. We need Gaia to raise our frequency, and She needs us to raise hers. It is a cumulative process, as light enters, more issues are dealt with, more healing takes place and more light can enter.

"The circumstances of individual lives of the Volunteers are as varied as human experience itself, but the Journey of the Volunteers has many parallels and similarities, the goal being that all aspects of the human condition are brought into an evolved and harmonious state.

"So you see, Amethyst, you were right when you set the premise for your story as a basic story of a generation of seekers. You are one of those Volunteers of the Seeker Status. By telling your own story and becoming aware of your healing process, you facilitate your own awakening. You also act as a catalyst in the awakening of others who will read your story and recognize the parallels in their own journey.

"Your memories and the story they tell are the REMNANTS FROM THE FIRE. You have endured the Alchemical Process wrought by the Fires of Transformational Grace, forging in you an awareness of your mission on Gaia and your Awakening."

Joriah went on to explain that originally their particular agreement had been to explore the process of waking up from being totally unaware and asleep to the experience of the first impulse of questioning through the long process and experience of gathering the threads of the tapestry of Awakening and weaving them with the experience of seeking.

"When you left to live on Gaia, aeons ago, you were emphatic about experiencing each step, each milestone along the way. You wanted to directly experience the pain and the ecstasy of physical life. You planned to live lives as both male and female, within a variety of belief systems. You set a course to directly experience and savor the joy of each discovery you made as a gradual process. You wanted to feel its impact on your body and your emotions.

"Before we parted, after the splitting apart you said to me 'I want to have plenty of challenges and obstacles to overcome, so make the forgetting effective, so that I can use the tension of limitation to push against. This will make the experience of separation deeply real.'

"So the polarities of desire and limitation were overlaid upon your psyche as you were born into the world on Gaia, and you began your long visit on the planet. The life you now live as Amethyst has brought you very close to coming home. You have traveled many lifetimes to arrive here.

"Gaia is so distressed that it is not yet known if She will continue to allow human life to inhabit her. As the Old One explained, there is a great deal of hope at this time, but the Great Awakening has to be accelerated to accomplish the work for the Grand Experiment to continue on a higher level of consciousness in cooperation with Gaia. Many like yourself, who have reached a point in their evolution of the process have the potential to accelerate their own awakening, and in the process become a worker for the planet's acceleration.

"You were being watched very closely, as we looked for an avenue in, to help you. You were guided into difficult circumstances in order to make you look harder for a way out. It was hard to endure from this side, watching you suffer, but we knew it was the only way. Remember, you had already been a seeker for several lifetimes and so we had permission to try and get you to respond.

"Many years ago in this lifetime, I heard your words, poignant, seeking, questioning. I felt your feelings of abandonment, loneliness, aloneness. I shed tears at your cries, for you are so brave, dear and precious to me. I constantly reminded myself of your parting wishes, because it was very hard to allow you to suffer. You did not have any knowledge of me, I had to find a way for you to learn of me. Even though I was an unknown part of you, I was allowed to reach through time and touch your heart.

"You have not figured this out yet, but your first guide was your grandmother. She is one of the Rememberers. She has been your guide and teacher in many of your lifetimes, under many guises. She loves you very much and agreed to come in before you and guide you to the work you would do, by insuring that your foundational development was heavily instilled with the desire to learn and the ability to question. She had great faith in your ability to handle the accelerated path.

"Later, by gently coaxing you along with the questions I tormented you with and through the answers you sought and wrote in your numerous journals, you discovered the answers to the clues set to trigger your searching.

"After your grandmother died, I sent guides to you who you would accept in The Old One and Lazaris. They worked with you, slowly raising your vibration until you were ready to meet me.

"Dearest one, how often I have wanted to reach down and pull you through the pain you were caught in, but I could not, for in the vibrations you held I would only have caused you harm. Your vibrations had to be raised slowly and through your own volition so as not to harm your physical vehicle. Your cries and begging made it hard to let you inch slowly along, but there was so much you had to learn to be ready for the responsibility that lay ahead of you if you were to succeed in completing the journey.

"I'll always treasure the time in meditation with Lazaris when we met for the first time. You could only see me as light, and yet we danced and you cried, and you knew you had experienced something important. Then you allowed me to manifest as Joriah, and we could become friends and get to know each other in such a deeply intimate way.

"In your meditations I would slip in, and you would recognize my presence as slight pulsating movement

166

throughout your body. I loved it as you became more and more welcoming to my presence inside of you. Little by little in changes and shifts so small they were imperceptible on a daily basis, you grew until the changes had altered you so completely even you recognized that you were not the same person who first snuck off to the Tower in despair.

"You were always headstrong with the willingness to risk by jumping off into the unknown. Often you would leap before you took a good look. You got yourself into plenty of scrapes but thankfully you were receptive to our guidance, and you were able to learn from your mistakes.

"You were so persistent and single minded in your desires that often you would manifest the desired outcome. I was pleased when you thanked me for my help. Pleased because you were not afraid to ask for help, and acknowledge it when you received it, and because you were learning to be a partner and co-creator.

"Know dear one, I did keep you on course through The Tempest. I couldn't comfort you, somehow you knew that. If I had comforted you, I would have stopped the process of release. Being in biological form is so tricky. By finding your way through The Storm you became strong enough to come out of it and shift to the next level.

"Little by little you began to grasp how to find your way along the path, your footing became steadier and your balance more accurate, and all the while you were getting stronger, so much stronger. I would rejoice when you would come to the place where you would 'get it' and ask for release, because at that point your request could be granted.

"I watched and waited as you faced and integrated the darkness in your psyche as you began to understand the projections that came out of that darkness. I marveled at the tenacity you showed in your drive to develop spiritually often pressing on even when you didn't understand why. Always, dear one I was right there just on the other side of the Veil of Forgetting sending you love and encouragement to balance the frustration and discouragement you often felt.

"Know that for every shaft of light you remembered and embraced there was great rejoicing on our side of the veil, for you were getting closer and closer to remembering and union. Now beloved one I stand before you as the doorway to your Future Self. After tonight I too will not be known to you by the form you now know me, for by the time this evening ends, you will have become me, and I you. It is time for us to merge, so that we can do this last part of the Path with our combined skills as conscious co-creators. You have grown enough that more Spirit can function in your body without harming it.

"No longer will you receive thoughts and inspiration from what you perceive as above, it will come from deep inside of you where I soon will dwell. You and others with the same yearnings have made the space for Spirit to come to the deepest parts of matter to transform it. You have made it possible to increase the amount of Spirit that can dwell inside a physical body.

"You are a part of me, and yet we are separate. Once split-apart we can never again come together in quite the same way, because our experiences have expanded us in immeasurable ways. In separateness you have gained strengths and skills, I can only witness. By joining you I bring knowledge of the world beyond the veils to the physical plane. Together we release the veils of illusion that have seemed to separate us, and we experience an exponential version of what we were before we split-apart."

As Joriah spoke, Amethyst sunk deeper and deeper into a meditative state. Joriah stopped speaking, and Amethyst felt her body fill with light and a gentle and powerful peace fill her being. She and Joriah were one.

***

Amethyst had reached the ultimate path, the path which would continue to take her deeper into the wholeness of enlightenment, the ultimate destination of all who participated in the Grand Experiment on Gaia.

She had given up the choice of the polarized plane, and when she did that, she was struck with the realization that choice between polarities was really quite limited. Now as the concepts of all that had just transpired sunk deeper and deeper into her consciousness, she realized that by choosing to give up choice for a greater cause, she was able to see how the polarities worked, and life beyond choice held great promise.

No longer subject to Archetypal projections, she could now apply the skills she had developed and acquired to the Great Work ahead, and love would be her strength. Nothing outside of herself could carry her this final way, she and Joriah would co-create as one. A chill of realization and exhilaration surged through her. Joriah had affirmed that all of her work through many lives had indeed been for a great purpose.

The Center of Light from her Divine Self that now filled her being would be her guide. She had succeeded in bringing a beloved portion of her Larger Self into matter. Feeling the Light of her Greater Self pulsate within her, she trembled with anticipation, wondering what lie ahead on this magnificent journey of consciousness. And she knew nothing would stop her now.

COAGULATION

"...results in a union of spirit and matter"

The Emerald Tablet
Dennis William Hauck

&

A NEW BEGINNING

CHAPTER NOTES

Introduction

1. **Tarot Correspondence Course**- My introduction to the symbolism and meaning of Tarot came from a correspondence course I took for about 2 years from The Builders of the Adytum, (B.O.T.A. Temple of Tarot and Holy Qabalah.) 5105 North Figueroa Street, Los Angeles, CA 90042 in the early 1980's. Their teachings are based on the symbolism of the Tarot Keys as they are depicted in the Ryder-Waite Deck. I will be forever grateful for the indepth and fascinating lessons on Tarot I received from them.

2. **Psychosynthesis**-Developed by an Italian doctor, Roberto Assagioli. His approach was to bring mysticism and psychology together into an integrative approach to personal growth and healing. The system is eclectic, integrating many principles and techniques to help the student go deep within himself developing both personally and spiritually. Dr. Assagioli saw man as having the tendency to grow toward harmony within himself. He is the author of *Psychosynthesis: A Manual of Principle and Techniques,* and *The Act of Will.* Dr. Assagioi died in 1974.

3. **Archetype**-The concept of Archetype is a fascinating one. I have discovered definitions of what an archetype is that run along a continuim from simple to extremely complex.

I will attempt to explain what I think an Archetype is, and my explanation is the context that I used to work with the concept in this book. I understand archetypes to be universal patterns of energy and influence that originate from the collective unconscious of all humankind.

I resonate with Jung's explanation of the collective unconscious as a field of consciousness that is shared with all humankind where patterns and symbols originate that influence each of us. Those patterns and symbols are archetypes. Many archetypal images are instantly recognizable in dreams, stories, and symbolic pictures, such as the wise old man or woman, father, mother, child, crone, witch, dragon.

Generally an archetypal image will generate some emotion for the person who is experiencing it. The emotional response will be individual. If someone has a good relationship with their mother for instance, that archetype in dream or picture will generate a positive emotional response. If the relationship was negative then the individual may react to that archetype with entirely different emotions.

Other archetypal images are not instantly recognizable, but show up in the dreams of educated and non-educated alike. They can appear in modern day dreams and be from an ancient era unknown to the dreamer. These images are shared by all.

AS an example Jung tells the story of a professor who had a sudden vision and thought he had gone insane. He consulted Dr. Jung in a panic, describing his vision. Jung took a 400 year old book from the shelf and showed him a picture of an old wood cut depicting his vision. It was a picture of archetypal images. (from *Man and His Symbols* by Carl G. Jung.) That is an example of a archetype coming out of the collective unconscious. It didn't originate with the person who had the vision, and had existed for hundreds of years. The next step with such a vision would be to explore that archetype and see what message it had to the person that had the vision. When people work with their dreams in depth, often they are exploring messages from the collective unconscious and the archetypal world.

When I speak of the Tarot Archetypes in this book, I am speaking of universal principles pictured by the symbols of the cards. Because they are universal principles or patterns of energy, they can influence each of us as we experience the dramas of life, and certain dramas evoke the archetype. They are recognizable patterns of influence and they come to us from the unconscious. Tarot personifies them, but in reality they are neutral, impartial forces.

We are usually not aware that we are acting out an archetypal drama. I am convinced that once we begin to recognize the pattern, we can influence the outcome and not be unconscious victims of the energy patterns.

I also think that new archetypes or prototypes come into being as we collectively agree on the meaning of an influence. When someone thinks of John Wayne or Marilyn Monroe we think of a certain type of person. We instantly see the pattern. We are recognizing an archetype of our generation.

When we use the life of the butterfly to symbolize the transformational journey of life, we are recognizing the archetypal pattern of transformation. If we realize that we will have a caterpillar stage of life, and time when we turn inward, the cocoon stage, and the time of transformation when we fly, we are seeing the archetype. We can move elegantly through the stages and not be frightened by them. If we don't understand what is happening in those stages, we are often terrified by them. The transitional time of going in and out of the cocoon stage, as well as the experiences while there can be a trying time for all concerned. Recognizing and understanding the process can help make the process more tolerable. If the process is allowed or encouraged, a transformation of the indvidual and/or an improvement in the life being lived can be the outcome.

The influence of archetypes is a mysterious process. Understanding that those influences exist has the potential to greatly enrich everyday experiences on the earth plane. The influences come from somewhere. That "somewhere" has been the catalyst to many a quest throughout history.

Prologue

1. **Lazaris** Lazaris is a channeled non-physical entity. They explain that They experience themselves on many levels and for that reason refer to themselves as We. It seems appropriate to me to refer to Lazaris in the plural as They do, thus the capital T on They. They channel through Jach Pursel. The company Concept:Synergy disseminates the Lazaris Material and sponsored Lazaris Seminars in many of the major cities in the United States as well as all over the world during the years this story took place. Jach no longer

travels, but he still channels Lazaris in Florida. For more information the mailing address is Concept:Synergy, Inc. PO Box 691867, Orlando Florida 407-876-4973 www.Lazaris.com.

Chapter One

1. **The Tower KEY 16** The Tower is the Archetypal symbol for awakening. It has parallels to the Tower of Babel, in that it symbolizes the destruction ofo the old form in order for a new form to emerge. In order to awaken, a confounding of the old belief structures has to occur, i.e. the old language. When one begins to come under the influence of the energy of The Tower it can feel like falling into a dark void of destruction, for life as it was known to that point is gone forever. The ego falls from it's perceived ruling perch.

At the same time, The Tower is a place of refuge, and like a light house, shines it's illuminating beam into the dark watery seas of the unconscious, searching for lost talents and hidden truths. The Tower can also be that place in the intellect where one retreats to sort out the dramas and issues of life.

The Tower represents a powerful and traumatic transition, and those brave enough or foolish enough or desperate enough to search for those forgotten stairs and climb them, will find themselves in a mysterious realm that will challenge them to their very core.

Chapter Two

1. **The Hermit KEY 9** The Hermit is the archetype of the Wise Old Man. He makes himself known in times of change and transition. He stands on the top of the Mountain of Enlightenment and shines the light of his lamp on the path up the Mountain, lighting the way for the Seeker. His arrival means that the Seeker has grown enough in The Great Work to have the courage to face oneself, and he imparts wisdom and knowledge to help the Seeker find the Way. His task is to share the Knowledge of the Mysteries, and to discern who is ready to receive them. He is a recluse, and work with him is accomplished in secret. He is a supportive companion as

one embarks upon the long, silent path inward and ascends to one's highest and deepest zenith of realization.

2. **The Fool KEY 0** The Fool is the archetypal representation of the Eternal Self. The begiinning and end of the journey. Each of the symbols of The Fool card represent an element of the mystery of life on the earth plane.

The sun in the right hand corner, symbolizes the radiant life force necessary to maintain life. The mountains in the background challenge the commitment of the seeker aspiring to ascend to higher consciousness; the melting snow the source of water to the fertile valleys below.

The Fool is on a cliff. He is accompanied by a dog, which represents the ego or intellect. At a spiritualized level, the dog represents the ego in cooperation with the Self, a faithful companion.

The figure is clothed in white undergarments representing purity, overlayed by a dark cloak signifying the forgetting of who we truly are, and covering ourselves with illusions. The fabric of the cloth is decorated with many representations of the cycles of nature.

The Fool stands on the precipice of illusion, ready to leap-the Cosmic Wanderer, The Self on an eternal adventure.

Chapter Three

1. **The Lovers KEY 6** This key has several dimensions to it. It is the archetype of decision, crossroads and choice and the polarities of yin and yang.The physical plane is a dance of polarities and The Lovers epitomize that dance. When The Lovers come to play in one's life, decisions and choices loom on the horizon and the familiar experience of life will never be the same. A turning point has been reached.

The Lovers hold within them the sacred power of attraction which exists between the polarities. Without this sacred attraction, life could not manifest in form. If one looks at the card as each figure being a part of one person, the female represents the inner reality or unconscious. She is looking up at the angel, who represents the superconscious, or Higher Self, or Source. The male represents the outer reality or physical human.

So we all have an inner part , the feminine principle and an outer part, the masculine principle. These represent a human who has the birthright, and the dimensions to look inward for help and guidance and answers. The unconscious of the person brings the answers in from the Higher Source, as we can see from the female figure looking up to the Angel. From a holographic point of view the card represents each human.

In the dance of polarities, The Lovers represents the attraction of male and female on the human level and all that entails, on the archetypal level the card represents each one of us as a whole being.

The Lovers Archetype links cause and effect with destiny. A conflict between idealism and materialism is inevitably generated with it's divine descent into earth form.

It is a complicated and multifaceted archetype, as complicated and multifaceted as life itself.

Chapter Four
1. **Secret Paths** *Women in the New Midlife* by Terri Apter 1995 W.W. Norton & Company, Inc. 500 Fifth Avenue, NY, NY 10110

Chapter Five
1. **Death-Key 13**-Death represents the archetypes of Scorpio and Capricorn, the polarities of expansion and contraction, release, letting go, rebirth and transformation.Capricorn, an earth sign reigns during the time of year when the earth sleeps, the sun is at it's weakest, and the days are short, so darkness predominates. Barrenness and death are everywhere. Capricorn is the archetype of the soul's imprisonment on the earth plane. The ego tries to master the world through Capricorn's intent. Since the ego fears death, as long as one is caught in the throes of the rigid, narrow life view of ego, death is seen as something to fear.

Scorpio represents the soul's journey through darkness and the transformation which is the result of that journey. It is a water sign, and water represents emotions. The Scorpio energy takes us to our deepest, darkest emotional waters. Scorpio is a catalyst that moves us through those dark waters and helps us transform the emotions, letting go of old outworn issues, so that we can be reborn.

(Personal note, I find it interesting that my sun sign is Taurus, my moon is in Capricorn and my ascendant is Scorpio. Perhaps it is the influence of those energies that drives me to explore and write about the expansion-contraction, letting go, rebirth and transformation process. Of all the Keys, I find the symbolism and process of what it represents the most fascinating.)

Chapter Six

1. **Pearl Diving** was the title given to the seminar she attended at Manna House. See below "Manna House" note 3.

2. See Psychosynthesis note # 2 in Introduction notes.

3. **Manna House** is an actual retreat center in Concordia, Kansas. It is operated by a group of nuns whose mission is to provide a retreat for people of all denominations to do spiritual work in a comfortable and nurturing setting. They provided excellent accomodations and the food was wonderful. It was truly a place for deep healing work to be accomplished.

4. **Maya** in the context of this poem Maya means illusion, and the physical world is the world of Maya or illusion.

Chapter Seven

1. **High Priestess KEY 2** The HIgh Priestess is the archetypal representation of subconscious mind. She holds the mirror that reflects our inner world back to us which serves as the bridge between the conscious and unconscious minds.

The High Priestess contains the hidden wisdom and secrets of the subconcious.

Once the traveler has arrived in the desert, through that part of the journey so often called the "dark night of the soul" The High Priestess can appear.

An initiation has taken place which prepares the Way for the recognition of Shadow. She guides the Seeker through the dark and murky waters of secret repressions, helping the Traveler to unveil mysteries which bring to light hidden facets of the soul's journey.

2. Initiation The word "initiation" used in this book means a new beginning. The ceremonies and teachings The Woman received were ceremonies specifically designed to shift her reality, and/or beliefs in some way and point her in a different direction.

Chapter Nine

1. **The Heirophant- KEY 5** The Hierophant is the archetypal representation of the inner teacher, and the principles of learning, wisdom and intuition.

The Hierophant or High Priest represents the drive behind the process of growth and learning. There is an inner force or drive that moves every living being on the earth to become what it is meant to become.

Anything received intuitively comes from the Inner Teacher. Stop and listen for that "still small voice" and the direction and guidance it has to offer. Any improvement we make in our lives, or in the lives of others comes from within us through that voice or force, which the Hierophant represents.

Where the High Priestess holds the mysteries and reflects our inner world, the High Priest drives us to action and instructs our progress.

Chapter Ten

1. **The Magician-Key 1** He is the Archetypal Principal of all possibilities. He represents the need for focus and concentration, the power of desire, and the necessity for order in the work of manifestation.

The Magician has the tools of creation at his disposal. He holds his right arm up, pointing the wand toward the sky, symbolizing that he is the conduit for the power which comes through the wand to him from above.

The cup or vessel holds water, which symbolizes emotion and feelings the catalysts of creation. The double edged sword signifies that for every construction, there is destruction; and the pentacle represents the elements of the physical world needed to complete manifestation.

Chapter Eleven

1. **The Turning Point** *Science, Society, and the Rising Culture* by Fritjof Capra 1982 a Bantam book published by arrangement with Simon and Schuster.

2. The quote is from an unpublished paper I wrote in college.

3. **The Empress KEY 3** The Empress is the embodiment of the Earth Mother Archetype, her names are numerous. Among them are Venus, Isis, and Demeter. Whatever her name, she is the Goddess of Love, Beauty and creative power, and symbolizes the process by which creative intelligence fertilized by imagination, brings forth its' progene onto the earth plane.

The Empress represents the feminine in all of her creative forms. She is the YIN energy, the Anima, the pregnant maiden, the mother. She is a marvelous mystery to comtemplate.

The symbols on the card of the Rider-Waite deck give us clues about the tools she uses in her work: the wheat represents nourishment or the life support system that makes it possible for us to live on this planet; the moon under her feet alludes to the mysterious lunar connection and cyclical nature of the female reproductive cycle. She wears the twelve stars in a crown around her head. They represent the twelve signs of the zodiac, the 12 months of the year in which all of nature cycles.

The Empress within each of us is the creative principle which conceives, gestates and brings forth ideas and life on this planet. She is the epitomy of the Taurus astrological sign.

Chapter Twelve

1. **The Emperor Key 4** The Emperor is the archetype of the masculine principle, and the mate of The Empress. Words and concepts that describe him include constituting intelligence, the creative word or Logos, order, reason,

action, the manifestation of the material world, and father, to name a few. He is the Yang energy, he is Animus.

He sits on a throne that is a cube. The cube represents the manifested world. The Key number is four. He commands the four elements to manifest creation. He is represented in profile signifying that part of what he does is hidden, he works in the veiled and unveiled worlds alike.

He corresponds to Aries, the first fire sign of the zodiac. Aries is the first fire of spring, the unfolding energy of germinating spring. The driving force of the will, the urge to act, and the spirit of enterprise are all part of the Aries energy and The Emperor. Aries is ruled by Mars the red planet. Red comes from fire, from the active energy of creation and of life living itself.

Chapter Thirteen

1. **The World KEY 21** The World is the Archetypal expression of the liberated World Dancer. This key represents freedom, liberation and self-realization. THe World Dancer is now ready to bring cosmic forces into expression in a personal way. The World Dancer has reached freedom, and is now ready to dance his/her's own dance. No longer subject to the choreography of other's ideas of how the dance should be performed, the World Dancer has arrived at the realization ot the unique dance of the Self.

The Dancer is surrounded by a wreath, life itself in the form of a victory wreath. It is elliptic in shape, and reperesents the womb where we develop and create the dance.

In the four corners of the card are the symbols of the fixed signs of the elements: the bull is Taurus of the element earth; the eagle is evolved Scorpio of the element water; the lion is Leo, the element of fire; and the human is Aquarius, and the element air, which is also intellect. All are the tools and gifts of earth, available for us to utilize in the creation of our dance.

About The Author

Lark Ferguson has been a student of consciousness studies and the human condition for almost thirty years. Her probings include an eclectic exploration of psychology, transpersonal psychology and metaphysical thought, as well as the study of the symbolism of Tarot, I Ching and the Runes.

During the early years of raising her six children she taught parenting classes through the local community college, Lamaze Preparation for Childbirth, and served as a Certified LaLeche League Counselor.

As her children grew, her interests took her in the direction of complementary medicine and physical transformation. By 1980 she had completed her training, and became a Licensed Massage Therapist, maintaining a private bodywork practice for sixteen years. During those years she taught numerous classes, including Yoga, Tai chi, Homeopathy and personal growth.

She earned her BA in Human Relations and has since worked as a Social Worker, Foster Parent Trainer and Public Health Educator. She lives in Nebraska with her husband.

She is currently working on a sequel to this book, *Stirring the Fires,* which will be an experiential workbook to aid explorers in stirring their own fires of transformation. The workbook is to be used in workshops where participants can work with the process to stir their own fires of transformation.

For information about having a workshop in your area the author can be contacted by email: landrferguson@aol.com

Printed in the United States
6012